D  e

Adria's
TRANSFORMATION

Studio Griffin
A Publishing Company
www.studiogriffin.net

Adria's Transformation. Copyright © 2023. Dr. Paula Y. Obie

All Rights Reserved. Printed in the United States of America.
No part of this book may be used or reproduced in any manner whatsoever without written permission except in the case of brief quotations embodied in critical articles and reviews.

For information, contact:
Studio Griffin
A Publishing Company
studiogriffin@outlook.com
www.studiogriffin.net

Cover Design by Ruth E. Griffin
Images by © Samuel B / Adobe and Jantanee / Adobe

This is a work of fiction. The events and characters described herein are imaginary. Any resemblance to actual events, locales, or persons, living or dead, is entirely coincidental.

First Edition

ISBN-13: 978-1-954818-38-5

Library of Congress Control Number: 2023931328

1 2 3 4 5 6 7 8 9 10

To the memory and legacy of my Mom,
the late Reverend Joyce L. Obie

Chapter 1
In the Restaurant

The bubbly, young waitress led Adria to the middle of the restaurant to a two-person table. Douglas called when she was in route to say he would be a few minutes late. The long-time friends had made plans to have an early dinner. Adria enjoyed Douglas' company as he was always consistent. Though she had moved away for a ten-year period, they continued to communicate or interact with each other several times a year. And this frequency seemed to suffice and assist with maintaining this type of connection.

Adria looked around her. She loved this cafe with its black and white checkered décor, ultra-soft napkins, and contemporary retro-atmosphere. The food was always tasty, the service great and the atmosphere not too stuffy. She could sit back, relax, and enjoy the experience. And the desserts! They tasted as if someone's grandmother worked all day and night to create the scrumptious sugary treats. It was a perfect place to hang out with friends and family and was one of Adria's favorite food spots.

Adria pulled out her cell phone but resisted the urge to read her emails. She did not want to get involved in anything to cause her to completely change her mood.

There were times she wished she could just unplug from the world, but she knew that would be the moment someone would really need her! Instead, Adria placed her phone faced up on the table and relaxed.

The waiter brought back her peach iced tea. She took a sip of the beverage then reached into her red satchel purse to locate the mineral powder compact to check her make-up and hair. After removing the shine from her face, she took a moment to look into the eyes of the person whom she had learned over the years to love and embrace.

The thirty-two-year-old image reflected at her revealed a much wiser, milk-chocolate brown-skinned lady with auburn and gold-streaked, shoulder-length hair. Her mocha brown eyes looked a little fatigued from working long hours, but Adria noted they were not as sad as during her times of grief and loss.

Her growth journey, which included ten years of living away from her hometown, developed her into someone she had envisioned but was not sure she would become. She liked this Adria, period. Was she perfect? No. But she liked her anyway.

She placed a lock of hair in its proper position alongside her face then decided to put it behind her ear. Adria smiled at her reflection. Her adulthood had taken her through a lot of scenarios—some she could verbalize freely and some she would keep close to her heart and never speak aloud. YES, she experienced some life situations that were not going to be verbalized by THIS Christian girl, as she knew some folks would just NOT understand her choices, AT ALL. The truth was, at times Adria did not know herself, or what drove her to make certain decisions.

Adria's Transformation

It took a decade away, after college graduation, to broaden Adria's horizons. It allowed her to just grow up and gain the freedom she felt she deserved. Her hometown had become too small for her daily life and the process of having people control her every move became exhausting.

When she left home suddenly, Adria's immediate goal was just to disconnect from everyone and give herself a moment to breathe some new air. And Adria did that, with almost no contact with her family members, except her Poppie and her brother Gerrard. After two years though, Adria started returning for birthdays and special occasions. Initially the visits home were brief, the special events allowing her to socialize with friends and family; and within that circle was Douglas, her childhood friend. He shared Adria's love for music and good food.

And when she wasn't there, because Douglas remained in Rockville, North Carolina, he would always ask someone in her family about her, particularly if he called and she did not answer him or return his phone calls in a timely manner.

Adria closed her compact and placed it back in her satchel. She took another sip of her peach tea, glanced down at her phone, and wondered how much longer Douglas would be stuck in traffic.

Within minutes, the hostess and Douglas arrived at the table sharing a good laugh. He sat across from Adria and gave her his normal greeting of, "Hello Gorgeous! I am sorry I am late! You look great, as usual!" Douglas added with a big smile as he complimented his friend and began perusing the menu.

Adria looked at him with an automatic smile. Ever since they met as teenagers, she always thought Douglas had the most beautiful soft-brown eyes. His left eye lid seemed to droop a bit and the curve of his eyebrow hinted at the implication of mischievous behavior. And he also had a gorgeous smile with the straightest and whitest teeth.

"Well, thank you, Sir," Adria answered cheerfully. "This has been a good week for me. The business is doing well, and the family has no major issues. Right now, everything seems to be okay in the Darden world."

Douglas ordered his beverage and drank from the water glass Adria had asked the waiter to bring for him when she first arrived.

Within just a few minutes the waiter returned with Douglas' glass of blackberry lemonade and both Adria and Douglas placed their entree orders. In the meantime, they munched on the contents of the new breadbasket placed in front of them.

"It was good to see your dad the other day at the birthday party!" Douglas stated. "All of you looked very happy. I love how you have so much fun together! And your mom is always beautiful! She looks younger every day!"

"My dad's really, really cool. It is good to see him happy again. Mama enjoys her birthday celebrations, and I am so glad she and I are in a much better place!"

Adria reflected briefly over the past fourteen months, and how much the family changed with the sudden death of Gerrard, her second oldest sibling. His demise impacted the dynamics of the Darden family forever. She dropped her smile temporarily as she thought of the road traveled since then. There were still days where the truth of his demise seems unbelievable—like a bad dream.

Adria's Transformation

Then she would visit his gravesite and stare at his black and gold marble tombstone and embrace the fact she would never be able to visit or talk to him on this earth ever again. For weeks after his transition, she would just drive to the gravesite and sit in her car, crying, trying to make sense of this new reality. Even now, her heart ached as she recalled the painful time in their lives.

Adria looked around the restaurant and then back at Douglas who was gazing at his phone. She paused her mental review of the brief reflection of those realities and took another deep breath.

Soon the waitress returned with Adria's seafood gumbo and Douglas' seafood alfredo.

"How was your day?" Adria asked.

Douglas shrugged his shoulders. "Today was good and I am glad to be off work early so you and I could hang out together. You know, someone said to me just the other day how different you looked since the last time they saw you!"

"Wow! I wonder, when was the last time they saw me?" Adria questioned. "Though I do feel like I have found my true identity. For a long time, I felt anger, confusion, and conflict and now I am no longer in a whirlwind."

Adria and Douglas met as teens at a musical gathering in their hometown of Rockville. She was just stretching out as a vocalist, and he had begun playing the piano and organ. The night was filled with music, conversation, and lots of hope for the future as the two became instant friends.

On the special home church events she attended, was when Douglas would also show up and they would chat. Douglas and her brother Gerrard became friends, and he was the one who kept Douglas informed of Adria's planned visits. Since her return home, their friendship had grown, and the reconnection was strong.

The two friends continued eating. They laughed easily and as always loved to share newsworthy information from their present and past. As they finished the entrées, drank their café lattes, and ate key lime pie, Adria became even more relaxed.

"I have a surprise for you!" Douglas announced. He then retrieved from his pocket a photograph and placed it in front of Adria. She picked it up and looked into the eyes of a group of high school friends who were smiling and posing for the camera. It was a much younger version of herself, Douglas among the group.

"Where on earth did you find this? Look at us!"

"What a fun night. We had such a good time!"

"The Senior Talent Show," Adria reflected. "I had to beg my parents to allow me to attend! I can't even remember how I got them to say yes. Probably because it was my senior year in high school. I had a copy of this picture, but I don't know what happened to it!" Adria reached for her phone and took a snapshot of the photograph.

"It was our debut!" Douglas laughed. "You know I have always loved to hear you sing. I thought you would do more with your gift, but you never did." He stopped briefly. "I mean, I thought maybe when you left us and stayed away, I would see you as a backup singer for some R&B group or something."

Adria continued to stare at the photograph; it represented a time in her life when music was important to her. Then one day it was not so important anymore.

Adria's Transformation

She looked up at Douglas, offered a slight smile and a deep audible sigh!

"I know, I know," Adria said. "Even on Senior Day, when I sang and got the standing ovation, I thought maybe this could be my calling or career, but shortly thereafter those feelings of melancholy just took over. So, I focused on getting my college degree as I felt it was the real vehicle for having a good life." Adria gave Douglas a strained smile as she took another sip of her coffee.

"Some people are not small-minded, and they need to live in a city with lots of possibilities. You are that type of person," Douglas shared. "I am a true country boy, and this town totally works for me! I don't think I could survive in a place much larger than this."

Adria chuckled at Douglas' admission of being a country boy. It was certainly part of his charming personality. Then she remembered he had a date last week.

"Now tell me more about this date you went on a few days ago. How was it?"

"It actually went pretty good," he responded. "She was a friend of a friend, and we talked about a lot of things," Douglas admitted.

"Any sparks?" Adria inquired as she smiled and made comical gestures with her shoulders.

"Yes, there were a few sparks flying around and some laughter!" Douglas responded. "We shall see!" Then without hesitation, he asked boldly, "Now, when are *you* going to come out of *your* shell and start dating?"

Adria offered Douglas a quizzical look and pursed lips.

"I just wanted to cocoon for a while—you know, spend quality time with me," she said.

"And what's the difference, between a shell and a cocoon, my dear friend?"

Silently Adria responded, "The butterfly to emerge," before saying aloud, "I have grown a lot, and I am very proud of this Adria. I've worked diligently to be the person I see in my own vision, and I am still not quite there yet."

"You are definitely on your way."

"Thanks. I am still learning how to keep myself on the top of my priority list and not allow other people's issues, problems or whatever, to always take center stage in my life," Adria declared.

"Well, again, from where I sit, you seem to have settled down pretty nicely, with a place to live, business partnership, and church," Douglas added.

"I am pretty comfortable."

"Are you having any more fun or just working hard?" Douglas asked boldly. "I mean you have been home over a year, my friend."

"It's been fourteen months and I don't regret taking this first year to just focus on me and my family, as there was so much sadness and transitions," Adria reflected. She looked down at her coffee. "Because of my grieving and loss periods, now I am extremely cautious of my vulnerability as it was how"—Adria hesitated momentarily—"Or when I drifted into a lot of messes in my past. I think most people can make pretty good decisions when they are not in certain types of transitions, like at the end of a relationship or suffering from constant disappointments or loneliness, or even grieving from a death of a friend or loved one. I was like a wide open sore though back then and I caught a lot of infectious people," Adria confessed. "I couldn't see, think, or feel clearly and

Adria's Transformation

I panicked, desperately in need of some type of relationship or attention. Most of the time I do attach to someone, and everything is different when I start healing. Then I feel guilty and try to make it work instead of being honest and ending the interactions. My whole family can relate to this type of decision-making, and it can be a dream-killer—even if we don't admit it."

Douglas nodded in agreement and added. "Yes, in those situations, we just don't want anyone to know how much 'do do' we stepped in. We are ashamed and embarrassed. And then God taps us on the shoulder to remind us who we are and gives us the courage we need to move forward."

"But some of us do not move forward and it's a big problem! Our Christian conscience kicks in and we feel guilty for being in that situation," Adria added. "Then we just keep making excuses. We just get stuck. You can only ignore being involved with the wrong person who doesn't love you the way you deserve to be loved in the right way for so long before it starts causing you a lot of problems in all areas. It's a very costly denial."

Douglas nodded slowly.

"And you know what else?" Adria said, "Those people don't usually have a lot to offer. In fact, when you look at it, they have more to gain from being with you than you being with them. But they catch you at the right or wrong time—the vulnerable time and you can't easily get away from them!" Adria's voice then drifted off.

She looked across the restaurant, then returned to look at her coffee cup as if it reflected her life's most precious scenes before she continued. The current song playing in the restaurant was 'Just Once' by James

Ingram and it set the perfect mood for this type of conversation. She continued.

"Like I've said many times before—and I am willing to talk to anyone who wants to hear it—I had a major meltdown. I poured my heart out to God and told Him how hurt I was and how my life was not what He promised me. I cried for Gerrard and his life! I got loud and cried hysterically. I kept asking God to help me, until I felt better. I wanted to no longer have my old way of thinking, or my anger, or my focus on childhood craziness, and losses." Adria's voice trailed off for a few seconds. "Then I heard God whisper to me and say, 'Trust Me.' I felt like I would be ok and be totally restored."

Afterwards Adria looked over at Douglas for a response. He had been gazing gently at her face before speaking. There were so many traces of her unhealed areas on display, and she had been talking for quite a while.

"So, now we just need to get you to keep loosening up and have a lot more fun. You are just way too serious!" Douglas laughed trying to change the subject and lighten the mood.

The waiter returned to refill her water. She let him finish before continuing.

"I have always been an intense person," Adria admitted as she drank from her glass of water. "Things are changing for me though, and I am doing activities I really enjoy, especially since I joined Greater Fellowship and the music ministry. I do love the chorale!"

"That's good to hear! I am so glad you are singing again," Douglas stated. "Your anointing is strong. I could feel it when I watched you sing at the concert a few weeks ago. Maybe this is the time to become the minstrel God created you to be. You just have to be open to allowing Him to put you in places to keep using your gifts," Douglas stated decisively. "And you are also going to need a man who is the type of companion to let you use it without going through a whole bunch of changes!"

"You mean like what Gerrard went through?" Adria asked sarcastically. It was more of a statement than a question.

"Precisely! You do not want to turn out like him. He wasted so much of his life when he deserved so much more!" Douglas reflected. "As musicians we would just wonder why he made his final companion choice. It just didn't make any kind of sense at all, and he did not live long after being with her!"

Adria's face became saddened again. She felt the familiar pang of hurt, even today.

Gerrard was Adria's second oldest brother who had tremendous musical talents. At one time it seemed he was headed in the right direction to use them to the fullest and realize his dreams. Then he just decided to remain in his current situation and not take advantage of the chances offered to him. Adria remembered him vocalizing his regrets on so many occasions. From her perspective, he never had a companion who celebrated his talents, but rather downgraded them or placed them lower on the priority list.

"I will repeat this every day if I have to, until someone finally gets the message. We"—Adria began and pointed her finger to herself—"make a lot of excuses for those folks who don't even deserve us!" Adria confessed. "It's like we are addicted and cannot get away from them!

"I guess we are just thirsty, in need of real love," Adria suggested. "Gerrard and I are so much alike ... we had dreams but couldn't find the companions to help us realize them.

"Unlike Gerrard, though, I ran as fast as I could when I had the chance. He wouldn't. He was afraid to live in a town across the country! I wished he could have at least tried, but he was just too fearful. I think it would have tremendously enriched his life and broadened his musical gifting."

Adria reached over to touch the ice glass and maneuver the liquid on the outside. This recurring topic was deep and the mood at the table became very intense—again.

Douglas lifted his water glass in a toast and announced, "Here's to fighting to move on to the next level in our lives!" Adria lifted her own water glass to tap his to complete the toast. Neither one of them noticed as two gentlemen walked over to the table.

"Hello Ms. Darden."

Adria looked up and recognized the two men. Standing at their table was the infamous Bryson Kenton, the Minister of Music at Greater Fellowship Community Church, or GFCC as they called it, who mesmerized audiences across the southern and northeastern United States with his college choir and small group performances.

The other man was Alton Brown, the choir director also known for whipping choirs into shape.

When Adria and Bryson locked eyes, she smiled and hoped her body language was not a true indicator of how she felt on the inside. To say she was taken with him would be putting it mildly. Bryson was handsome, with

Adria's Transformation

caramel colored skin tone and a strong square facial shape with a closely shaven beard. His eyes were deep set and mocha brown, and a signature smile of straight orthodontist teeth. She and Bryson had spent time together casually but hadn't had any one-on-one time in two and a half weeks, though for good reason.

"Well, hello there!" Adria responded. "Bryson and Alton, do you know Douglas?" She quickly introduced the two church members to her friend and diligently worked to remain calm and focused on her social skills and her manners. Her insides, though, was a totally different reality. They felt like milk chocolate melting in a stainless-steel pot over a heated stove. She was not prepared to see him today! And certainly not with Douglas around. The awkward feeling in her stomach was calmed though when she forced her eyes away from him and focused her attention on Alton.

"I recognize Douglas from the concerts. Nice to meet you." Bryson reached out to shake Douglas' hand, and like a Southern gentleman Douglas stood to meet the greeting. He then afterwards reached out to shake Alton's hand.

Bryson looked briefly at Adria and then at the hostess who was waiting to lead them to their dinner table.

"Well, we just wanted to say hello to you two! Our table is ready, and I am starving. Talk to you later. Nice meeting you, Douglas!"

The uncomfortable feeling in her core was almost too awkward to hide. She placed her hands in her lap and sat straight in the chair, trying to give the outward appearance of calm, and wondered what on earth caused them to choose this restaurant on this afternoon. After a moment, she refocused her attention back to Douglas, who looked directly into her eyes.

☙

Bryson and Alton made sure the hostess seated them in a corner where Adria and Douglas were not visible. The waitress appeared and they placed their beverage and entree orders. Bryson presented a nonchalant face and body language as he knew Alton was watching him, looking to catch his reaction after seeing Adria with her friend Douglas.

"Adria looks great," Alton offered. "Do you think she is serious about this guy?"

Alton and Bryson met in their college music theory class and became instant friends. Their camaraderie through the years continued to grow as Alton supported Bryson in all his musical endeavors. They were the same age and regarded each other as brothers. Their musical acuities and interests were similar and made them inseparable. Alton was not always happy with Bryson's choices, but he tried to remain an honest and faithful confidante and advisor.

Bryson shrugged his shoulders and sipped his water. "I don't know. She's mentioned him casually, and he has been around often in the past few weeks."

"I *thought* he was the same guy," Alton responded nodding his head favorably. "He has been to all of our concerts lately and a couple of other church engagements. I think I heard him sing at a banquet once. He has a nice voice."

Bryson remained stoic and attempted to conceal his reaction, but the truth was he could feel the jealousy

Adria's Transformation

stirring in his chest. He was powerless to stop it though. He took a piece of ice in his mouth and swished it around in an attempt to numb his senses and stop the unexpected 'envy monster' from swelling and growing uncontrollably. He could only hope that his truth was not showing on the outside.

Alton answered the question for him with the next response.

"You know, she's been watching you a lot lately and when she looks at you her eyes soften. There are times when you are singing, and your eyes are closed, and she has this 'look.' It's a tender gaze and says a lot if you were paying attention and purposely looked."

Bryson did not speak but accepted Alton's response as an indicator that his true feelings were on display. He took another sip of water and grabbed a larger piece of ice. Perhaps two pieces would stop the gnawing sensation in his abdomen which was tightening by the minute.

The two of them chatted about upcoming music ministry activities. After a while, their food arrived.

"Here's our food," Bryson stated, thankful for the waiter's timing.

"I did not expect to see her here today," Bryson stated before he picked up a chicken wing and silently, continued the thought, "And certainly not with him."

"I understand," Alton responded after he said grace over his food and then began to eat from his own chicken wing platter.

"I know you are not asking me for advice, but I'm your friend and have known you for a very long time. You have fallen for her, but you have not told her. I think she has fallen for you and not told you. When are you two going to be honest with each other?"

Bryson glanced at his phone as if he were searching the device for answers. Then he took another bite, wiped his mouth, and decided it was time to initiate this conversation. Alton was the only guy he would talk to.

Bryson used his fork to move his food around his plate before speaking, "Is it that obvious ... I mean my feelings?"

"To the world ... no. To me, yes," Alton replied. Bryson did not respond but looked up as Alton reached for a celery stick to dip in the sauce mixture/concoction he created on his plate.

Bryson gazed at his phone instinctively, as if he were expecting to receive a text from Adria. He then turned his phone face down and made sure the sound was turned off.

"I can tell just by the way you respond when she walks into the room. You are tough on our singers, and on our lead vocalists, you are even tougher. In the last lead vocalist's rehearsal, something happened during her song. I watched you ... something was happening to you... you were nicer!"

Bryson listened to Alton and offered no immediate response, except to continue to eat his veggies and entree.

"Did you know there are times when you actually walk away if she joins the group? It is kind of a subtle action, and you always busy yourself with the keyboard or the music. It's like you can't get too close to her. Now, why would you walk away every time unless something was going on between you two that was more than a casual ministry connection, that you are maybe trying to hide?" Alton used his hands to emphasize the impact of his words. He raised his hands in the air, in the "why" or "Y" position.

Adria's Transformation

Alton stopped for a moment to regroup, before asking, "So, what is going on between you two?"

Bryson looked up and replied courteously, "We have gone out and always had great conversations. We laugh and talk, and she was always warm and friendly."

"Have you kissed her?" Alton asked enthusiastically. "You can tell a lot about your feelings when you have the kiss!"

"Yes, we have kissed, and held hands," Bryson admitted, "But there has only been one real serious kiss." Bryson quickly responded and then smiled broadly before adding, "And it was a good kiss. My lips tingled afterwards." Bryson reminisced on the serious kiss as it happened just a couple of weeks prior before she backed off and stopped communicating as often. It was a great evening, and he looked forward to them going out again.

"I think you need to talk to her and be honest. What are you afraid of?" Alton asked boldly, shrugging his shoulders for emphasis.

Bryson reached down to choose another item from the platter before responding.

"I didn't think I was afraid of anything. I just don't know if I want a serious relationship right now. You have to work too hard."

"It's been over five years since you and Rheta were engaged. And Adria is not like Rheta at all," Alton replied, glancing up at Bryson.

Bryson and Alton talked about Rheta sporadically as it was known how much he loved her.

"And those girls you have been going out with...well, you just don't seem to be really into them at all," Alton resumed. "With Adria, I don't think you would have to work hard as she does not seem like a drama queen."

"At first, Rheta wasn't a drama queen and then she changed when she was pregnant with Duane," Bryson said, then added, "Her personality shift came out of nowhere. She wasn't the same person I fell in love with."

"This is true, but that doesn't have to be your last love. I'll tell you what, Adria can sang, and she is truly anointed. When she sings, I get chills down my spine and go right into worship. I have heard nothing but good things about her; she seems to be a woman of integrity. When are you going out again?" Alton inquired.

"We talked about once or twice a week and have mostly seen each other at choir functions, group dinners or outings."

Bryson hesitated as he was not certain he wanted to be one hundred percent transparent with Alton. He looked around the restaurant to be sure neither Adria nor her companion was not in ear shot.

"Remember the night we sung 'Hold On' at our pastoral anniversary evening service and the chorale had the house from the first stanza? There was not a dry eye in the place and the Holy Spirit fell like rain on all of us, especially her. We danced for a minute after that song. First Lady ran around the church and the ushers could not get her to calm down!"

"Yeah, I remember. We had a nice time that night," Alton agreed.

"I watched Adria in worship, and it was like she gave it everything she had, withholding absolutely nothing and did not care who was watching," Bryson reflected. "I don't know, it really impacted me." He used one of his hands in an upward motion for emphasis.

Adria's Transformation

"Okay!" Alton stated. "But just keeping it real, a lot of us were in true worship that night and the chorale was wrecked!"

"Exactly. The rest of us went out to eat and she decided at the very last minute not to join us. I walked her to the car, and I asked if she was sure she didn't want to hang out with the gang and she said, *'No, I'm a little wiped out',*" Bryson said.

"Uh huh," Alton responded.

"The whole time all of us were at dinner, I just could not stop thinking about her. It was also the same night Diane started acting weird towards me and being extra attentive!"

"Diane always knows when to give you extra attention," Alton interjected, "I am just saying!"

Bryson ignored Alton's comment.

"Diane got a bit too cozy, and I told her to chill out, but since that night Adria has backed off too. We've talked but it was casual. It's almost as if she got scared or something. I wonder if someone said anything to her about Diane and me."

"Humph," Alton responded, slowly nodding his head. "Sounds like it. When she came to rehearsal on last Thursday, I noticed she was a bit standoffish and was sorta watching Diane. If you remember, Diane was especially 'friendly' towards you at rehearsal too. Maybe she thinks the two of you are an item."

Bryson looked up at Alton as if he had just been enlightened. "That's it! That's it!" He lifted both hands in the air and leaned back in the chair. "I have been trying my best to figure out what caused her to become so chilled these past couple of weeks. She must think I am not being honest with her about Diane."

Alton shook his head affirmatively. "So, what do you do? You two are not dating each other exclusively."

"No, we are not really dating at all, but we've had great times together," Bryson said.

"Those great times you have had together are called dates Bryson. Just how many times are we talking about?"

Bryson ignored the question, and instead said, "There's a song I want her to learn before our next rehearsal. This gives me a reason to check-in and then we can talk about this face to face, I guess," Bryson stated hesitantly.

Alton nodded his head. "Yeah, dawg, but what if this thing really gets serious? Are you ready for it? She is the type of lady you could fall hard for! Really, really hard! I mean, if I were not married, I would be trying to get to know her myself!"

Bryson glared seriously at his friend. Then he looked around the restaurant in the area in which Adria and Douglas were sitting. He could not see their table but wondered if she was enjoying her company. He was not certain how to respond to Alton's questions.

"I don't know what I am ready for," Bryson admitted.

గ్ర

Adria and Douglas were enjoying another cup of coffee as they chatted about his upcoming event in Washington D.C.

"You should come with us; we could stay an extra couple of days and do the sightseeing thing." Douglas suggested enthusiastically.

Adria's Transformation

"I can't leave town right now. I'm pretty busy with church activities and my business," Adria stated.

"Oh yeah, you are a part of the Chorale!" Douglas remarked sarcastically.

Adria smiled. "Yes, I am." She picked up her cell phone to quickly view an incoming text message, almost expecting the text to come from Bryson.

"I guess you won't have a lot of time to do anything else," Douglas teased.

Adria ignored Douglas' comment.

"So, tell me more about Bryson then," Douglas inquired changing the subject.

Adria reached around to adjust her purse on the back of her chair. She glanced towards the area where Bryson and Alton were dining. Once she confirmed their table was not visible, Adria spoke:

"He's a powerhouse praise and worshiper and I love his music and he is a great singer. He writes a lot of the music we sing but is not opposed to singing the latest and greatest tunes."

Adria tried not to disclose her true feelings about Bryson, but unbeknownst to her, her face beamed, she became less matter of fact, and more jovial. The truth was she was head over heels about Bryson. She had grown very fond of him, but she was not comfortable yet revealing her real feelings for him and not sure how he felt about her. She was not going to set herself up for anymore disappointments. Adria told herself time and time again she did not desire to complicate her life; however, she felt there was something between them, and each time they were together it was growing stronger. But nothing had been verbalized aloud, so there was no point in saying anything. It just felt like a sea of emotions.

"Has Bryson ever been married?"

"No, why do you ask?" she inquired.

"Just curious. He seems like a perfect match in many ways for you, my Cherie!"

Adria was taken somewhat aback at his boldness but simultaneously welcomed the chance to further explore the subject. "Based on what?" she asked raising her eyebrows dramatically.

"He's a godly man, musically talented and successful. He's also very nice looking. I think you two will look great together," Douglas remarked.

She looked up at Douglas attentively. Although she did not plan to have this conversation today about Bryson, she remained receptive and wanted to continue.

"Okay! Now it's your turn, tell me what you know about Bryson."

Adria positioned her head sideways to indicate she was open to hearing what he had to say. The look was a typical Adria gaze she used in her adulthood to show she was laser focused on the person speaking.

ങ

Douglas cleared his throat before continuing.

"Most musicians follow each other's musical journeys. I have followed him from the sidelines down through the years. And when you joined the church, and the choir, I started asking even more questions. Overall, he seems to be a good guy and you should snatch him up, gorgeous!" Douglas concluded.

Interesting, Adria thought silently. She settled back in her chair, lifted her head slightly.

"It's obvious he has not found a woman suitable to be his wife. You could very well be the one who steals his heart," Douglas adds. "Now, he has been connected with some very pretty girls, but the relationships never lasted long."

"Really?" Adria responded.

"Yes, really. Maybe he was searching for a very special woman? Now the grapevine reports he was a bit of a womanizer, but there are always rumors like that. I wouldn't put too much stock in those," Douglas said with a smirky smile.

Adria's only response was to chuckle softly and shake her head slowly. She had witnessed firsthand experiences with her family members musicians', and ministry attractions. The conversations from Mama and Papa Darden to their offspring were a constant warning of the consequences of their careless or casual sinful actions. Their warnings often fell on deaf ears and the liaisons turned into situations which at times needed their intervention.

"What exactly do you mean by a womanizer?" Adria probed further.

"You know as well as I do, any time a single or even married, male musician walks into a room, the single and even some of the married ladies, take notice. They stare and then offer their invitations. Some men can resist their requests, and many have no problem with the advances," Douglas added. "It's just the way it is!"

Adria offered an affirmative nod and remained silent. She stared at Douglas as she pondered all the types of advances Bryson may have accepted along the way.

"When you two locked eyes earlier, I was watching. If you are into him, and you two become a couple and you choose to be happy then I am in your corner," Douglas stated. "I also recommend you take it slowly," he also suggested. "Take the time to get to know him and find out who the real Bryson Kenton really is."

Adria glanced up at Douglas as ten years of experience flashed quickly before her eyes. *Oh, if you only knew,* Adria thought to herself. "I am not as naïve as I used to be," Adria admitted.

Adria looked beyond Douglas before speaking and prepared herself to share even more of her truths. She placed her hands on the table in an interlocking position.

"I have not felt this way in a long time or maybe ever! It's like I just looked around and Bryson was there. I attended an afternoon service where Greater Fellowship was the guest church and instantly connected with Bishop's message and the choir. Then I visited the church for a month before I became a member."

"You have been attending there a year, correct?"

"Not quite a year yet. I walked up to Bryson the morning I joined the church and introduced myself. He recognized me and we exchanged phone numbers."

"Have you been out?" Douglas inquired.

"Yes, we have been out, more so after I joined the choir—we talk a lot about music," Adria confessed. "It's nice to be around someone you like and who shares your passions. But when I heard him really minister the first time, I saw everything in a man I wanted, even if it was not him. I guess I am a little afraid of pursuing it ... afraid of messing it up. My track record isn't the best."

"True, but it's your past sweetie. Have you heard from J lately?" Douglas inquired cautiously as she had only shared with him a little bit of her relationship with the man. He did not attend Gerrard's homegoing service but sent flowers. Adria showed Douglas the beautiful flower arrangement in the shape of the letter "G" and beautiful house plants he sent along with a very heartfelt card. Adria also did not disclose to anyone J sent her money to assist with Gerrard's final arrangements.

"Every so often he checks in, but that's all," Adria said. "He says he just wants to see how I am doing. And there is absolutely no comparison between J and Bryson."

"Understood. I do think your present and your future are ahead of you. In fact, here comes your future now," Douglas pointed out as Alton and Bryson headed toward their table.

Adria prepared herself for another interaction.

"You all take care now," said Bryson, as he walked by. Adria could not resist gazing at him for a few seconds.

Alton smiled and replied, "See ya' later."

"Bye-bye," responded Adria as she waved her hand and smiled. Douglas lifted his pointer finger in their direction, flashed his 'Douglas' smile and stated, "Later, Man!"

Then he turned his attention back to Adria. "How long are you going to deny how much you are into this guy? You deserve some type of happiness and if he makes you happy, then go for it."

"Easier said than done my friend, easier said than done." Adria answered.

"When he walked by, he was looking at you with a purpose. You should take the lead and if it works out then you can take the credit for showing courage."

"And if it doesn't work out?" Adria inquired seriously.

"Then I'll be right here as always," Douglas stated boldly, and she knew he meant every word.

Dr. Paula Y. Obie

Chapter 2
Let's Get Real

After leaving the dinner with Alton, Bryson's ride home was not very pleasant. All he could think of was Adria and Douglas together at the restaurant. She told him they were childhood friends, but he was suddenly insecure and unsure of himself.

In all honesty, he had no right to react in this way at all since he had not made any attempts to admit his real feelings to himself or Adria. After the passionate kiss two weeks earlier, he fell hard for her!

Since then, there had been more than one opportunity to loosen up and give her a call to go out again. But he felt it best to follow the perspective of keeping his emotions hidden and not act on them. Those types of kisses could get you in a sexual situation faster than you could blink an eye...and he had the experience to prove it.

Maybe if he were extremely honest with himself, Bryson did not feel worthy of her. She was serious about her relationship with God and flowed with a powerful anointing when singing. Maybe, just maybe he was not feeling up to par and that's why he hadn't called her. She was different than all the others.

Since joining the ministry at GFCC, he faced the challenges of having the reputation of being a lady's man. First, he walked into the Minister of Music interview session having to defend himself to the church board as to why he was an unwed father. He communicated with the board members, who consisted of both men and women, it was his plan to get married. He even proposed and was preparing for his upcoming wedding ceremony, but he had to reveal that his relationship became so toxic he decided to end the wedding plans to focus on being the father his son, Duane, deserved.

He would have thought this type of interview would have caused him to be a lot more cautious when he started dating again. However, realistically, Bryson found himself in the careless situation of going out with more than one woman at GFCC. He reflected on the amount of attention he received when he joined the church staff. It was unbelievable how often his phone would ring after choir rehearsals or a church outing and the number of invitations he received to "hang out." A few of those women, even if it was just dinner and a movie, would contact another woman and tell her the details of the outing. In addition, some of these women shared stories of their intimate and sexual encounters. Although he insisted he was not sleeping with all those women, his deteriorating reputation became very problematic. He was reprimanded by the GFCC church board and the Bishop to "clean up his behavior or lose his job."

It was hard for Bryson to embrace how even though some of the stories were untrue, they were easily believed. He also had to accept the truth that some of those dates also included some type of sexual activities. Bryson was no saint, and he knew it. Still, he initiated the process of changing his behavior and trying to diligently remain loyal to God, to family and to his church. He failed many times, but he continued trying, nonetheless.

Bryson adjusted the satellite radio music to better listen to one of his favorite classics. The lyrics were appropriate as it asked the *"Holy Spirit to speak to our hearts with a message of love to encourage me."*

Earlier, Alton urged Bryson to be truthful about his feelings for Adria. What exactly was his truth? Was this real love or infatuation? Was he intimidated by her somehow? Maybe it was because she seemed too perfect for him? Or maybe because she was also part of a great family from their former general church organization that he had known since his childhood?

"Who knows? This could be the woman I have been searching for. She actually could be the one." His thoughts were non-stop and racing at the rate of his speedometer.

Bryson had not realized how much Adria had gotten his attention or how much she had penetrated his heart – until he saw her this afternoon with another man.

꩜

Bryson found himself driving near the Carrington-Tate Mall and made the decision to stop in and go for a walk. The mall was always a great place to unwind and to be productive. He wrote one of his most impactful songs while ambling through the corridors of the mall and in and out of his favorite stores. The words came first and then the tune. By the time he walked to his car, the song was written and only needed a few tweaks before he shared it with the church's music ministry.

As he strolled through the main glass doors, down through the shining mall corridors and onto the escalator, he allowed his thoughts to continue to flow freely and randomly.

"Let's see," Bryson reflected silently. He knew of Adria as a teenager since their families attended regular church conventions and events together. However, he was just now really beginning to get to know the adult Adria. After visiting GFCC in September last year, she became a church member in November. It had been about eight months since the Sunday she introduced herself to him. With his encouragement, she decided to join the music ministry.

And for the past two months, they spent time in each other's presence both personally and musically.

Even though he and Adria had been out a few times one-on-one, they mostly socialized in a group setting. It was a choir tradition to eat out after some rehearsals and after their renderings. They were a strongly connected group; some participants even developed close relationships. Many of the choir members considered each extended family. These social times were almost as important as the singing or church event.

At their last personal one-on-one outing, Bryson and Adria kissed for a long time. They had kissed before, but this one was different. This kiss was passionate, not hurried, affectionate and with follow-up kisses. Each time she was warm and reassuring; and smiled afterwards. She seemed to be becoming more and more comfortable with him.

It had been about two and a half weeks since that date and it caused him a great deal of difficulty later. Bryson simply could not stop thinking about her. It was not unusual for his mind to have thoughts of the girl he had been intimate with as it was a natural physical reaction. But he was having this type of effect after a deep, sensuous kiss. It was a sign, and he knew it. Adria had penetrated his heart and the kiss was the key placed in the lock. He just could not get her out of his head!

So, it had been puzzling to him why she had backed off. In his conversation with Alton today, he realized it might have been because of Diane. But the truth was Adria could have been approached by any lady in the church whom he had dated wanting to share their interactions with him. Bryson had lately tried to ignore the number of texts and phone calls received after rehearsals or church events with tempting invitations. However, he would admit at the onset of his appointment, for a time, those texts or phone calls did not get ignored. It fueled into the reputation he had today! And Adria could have been exposed to that.

Each time he and Adria interacted at church, in a church group or alone, the key was turning the lock and opening the door of his heart. The fact that he was envious of her, and her friend Douglas was another sign the size of a billboard he could no longer ignore.

Bryson took the 'up' escalator to the third floor where the more exclusive shops were located as the silent self-talk continued.

"Well, I guess I have to admit I am in love, but what in the world do I do with it? How long will this one last?" he silently mused. "The last time I was really in love was over five years ago with Rheta and it didn't turn out as I expected. Lord, please help me! I am not sure I am in the mood for this!"

Bryson automatically strolled into his favorite jewelry store, Marques' Jewels, and began to browse. This is the jewelry store where he purchased birthday, Christmas and other special gifts for himself, his family members, and special friends. The store owner knew Bryson personally and immediately started a conversation. Bryson referred many of his friends and associates to shop in this jewelry store.

"Hello Bryson, my friend!" Marc greeted Bryson as he walked in. "It's been a while since you have been here!"

"What's up, Marc?" Bryson responded.

"I have some great new things to show you!"

"I am just looking around today. I'm not in need of anything specific but let me see what you have new."

Bryson followed Marc around the counters where the watches and cuff links were displayed. Then beautiful diamond and gold tennis bracelets and necklaces. The two men slowly moved towards the right to the area where the female and male diamond rings were displayed. Then Bryson saw it—a heart-shaped ring surrounded with baguettes diamonds which sparkled under the light. It was incredibly gorgeous, and he could not resist asking to inspect it. Marc obliged.

The diamonds were perfectly set, and the ring was the right size for any type of hand. But Bryson was only thinking of one set of hands—the one he held as they walked through the park, the mall and as they rode in his car.

Bryson pondered on the timeline of his last interaction with Adria. She had not been as responsive and after today he had a greater insight as to why. So, the real question was, should he purchase the rings?

"This is crazy!" He thought immediately. Because, of course, the ring set was on sale.

After thinking about it, Bryson justified the purchase, knowing he could always exchange it for something else, if things did not work out in his favor.

"What am I doing?" Bryson asked himself sternly. "Have I lost my mind?" What sane person purchased a ring after just a few events? Had he decided this relationship could be less casual and more serious?

Maybe the real truth was he wanted it to become serious. Maybe the truth was he was growing tired of dating many women to find the right one. Maybe what God was trying to tell him was He had brought to him the woman he was praying for. And Lord knows, he had been praying, Bryson silently admitted.

For the last few years, Bryson felt the strong urge to settle down. Many of his friends were getting married, having families, and enjoying their lives. He and Rheta began dating and within one year, he proposed marriage and gave her a ring. As he and Rheta were sexually active prior to their marriage, she became pregnant. He had a son, Duane, who was his little prince; and although he got the 'cart before the horse,' he adored his son and legacy. Unfortunately, the relationship with his mother, Rheta, did not work out.

Bryson really did love Rheta and tried everything in his power to overlook her behavior. However, when his family was forced into the chaotic and unbalanced conduct, he knew he had to face facts. Something had gone wrong with his fiancé emotionally, so he decided they would marry after Duane's birth, and she had been given time to heal. As Rheta's behavior did not improve, it was his sister Tara who intervened.

Tara encouraged Rheta to seek professional assistance to enable her to become the mother and the future wife both her son and future husband deserved. Rheta denied needing any assistance and eventually the marriage plans ended. Now, four years later, they were both good parents and only interacted when it involved their son Duane.

Bryson was coming to the realization maybe God sent to him Adria to be his companion for life. This would explain why his marriage plans with Rheta ended so drastically.

Bryson wondered if she felt the same way about him.

"Lord, I sure hope so. If not, I am getting ready to truly reap some of the stuff I have sown!"

With no other ring set comparable to the pink and white heart-shaped diamond baguettes ring set, his decision was final.

Twenty minutes later he walked out of Marques' Jewels with the ring set in his jacket pocket. He basked in the great feeling of accomplishment. As he walked through the mall and towards his car, he was almost giddy and very proud of his decision.

This time the drive was a lot more enjoyable. He was not as anxious and much less desperate.

Chapter 3
Truth?

Adria and Douglas finished their dinner, and she was finally on her way home. The two friends chatted about everything from musicals to church events and family topics. However, the high priority discussion—Adria's interest in Bryson—was where the conversation ended. Adria was now thinking even more deeply about the possibilities of their future as a couple.

It was her desire to keep her feelings for Bryson discrete for as long as possible. Adria was not ashamed of Bryson, but she understood he had a high profile, and things could get crazy and chaotic if she revealed too much too soon. Normally, Adria would not have discussed her feelings with anyone this early in the relationship. She was accustomed to holding these topics close to her chest. The ability to step out of her very closely guarded box today took a lot of courage and energy. But she felt relaxed enough before to have this discussion with Douglas.

It was ironic for Bryson and Alton to decide to eat at the same place as she and Douglas and when her eyes met Bryson's, Douglas was watching and saw her feelings revealed. This made it much easier for her to share her heart with Douglas. It was certainly unplanned, but the conversation gave her even more hope. She admitted the next step was going to be risky and require a great deal of bravery. Adria was unsure if she could employ the type of boldness needed to be the first one to express her true feelings as Douglas suggested. That's why she had pulled away from Bryson—she was just plain scared. She was frightened of the thought of getting hurt. But if she didn't take a risk, she would never know if what they had was real, if it was worth pursuing.

Adria thought about Bryson and the look in his eyes as he said goodbye on his way out of the restaurant. He was clearly bothered, and she wanted to fix it. As it was, this was real for her, but the truth was, she always wanted to fix things, even if it was not necessarily the right thing to do. Adria's 'Ms. Fix It' attitude brought her some agony and shame in the past and she couldn't use it to gauge her current situation.

"What would be the disadvantage if I did call Bryson first, though?" Adria asked herself aloud. They were both adults and therefore did not need to play games. Was this behavior against the social rules?

Adria exited onto the freeway and used the car's cruise control feature to continue her excursion. Adria drove for several miles, then exited onto Highway 584, and made a right-hand turn onto Sedonia Drive. She recognized she was just driving around aimlessly and decided to turn into the neighborhood playground. Bryson and Adria walked in this park on one of their outings and she saw it as a good place to stop and regroup. Hopefully, she would find the encouragement needed to make the phone call to Bryson.

Adria's Transformation

Adria backed her car into the first parking space and gazed out the window to view her surroundings. The park was well-manicured, complete with two shelters and park benches, outdoor grills, with plenty of space for picnics, playing a game of frisbee or just relaxing.

She wasn't relaxed now, though. Adria sighed and stared at her phone for a while as she pondered her next step. She finally picked it up and held it in her hand.

"Douglas was right," she told herself, "I really need to make the first move to break the ice and if it backfires, then, oh well, at least I had the courage to try!"

Adria located Bryson's name and started to tap it, but she could only stare intently at his information. She blinked her eyes slowly. The same type of paralysis she felt in the past, causing her to not take charge of her life at key times, gripped her. As she continued to gaze at his phone number, she reflected on the conversation about him being a womanizer. She also thought about her relationship with J, who was an admitted ladies' man, and how she accepted his behavior at that time.

At that time...

It did not bother Adria to have his other girls around while she served drinks as a cocktail waitress and then eventually as one of the club bartenders. Adria knew she was J's Number One Girl and so she merely disregarded the other women. Sometimes, she was insecure, but J always had a way of helping her feel even more special than the others. Truthfully, with J, she knew what she was getting involved in. So, what was different now?

Adria had undergone a myriad of changes since her relationship with J ended. She did not desire to resuscitate the type of woman she was when she was involved with him. It was her goal to keep the former Adria 'buried' in the place she had left far behind her. At times, she glimpsed at the Adria in the rearview mirror of her life. The loss of J was sudden and impacted her emotionally, but not nearly as much as losing her dear brother. Gerrard's loss jolted her. It shattered her emotionally and motivated her to move home as quickly as she could to be near her family.

Also, she had been in fervent prayer about direction for her life as her relationship with God was re-established. She knew having a relationship with God did not grant her great social skills or guarantee she was going to have a healthy love life. Adria understood that it was possible to have a great anointing and be involved in a verbally, emotionally, and mentally abusive relationship or marriage. Given her experience, she needed God's direction for her life, and all of this was just a reminder to keep pushing forward. This woman now lived in a totally different world from the one in the rearview mirror.

Adria continued to stare at the phone. She acknowledged she had deep, deep feelings for Bryson. If she was being totally transparent, she could admit she was in love with him. However, today she admittedly didn't have the boldness to make this type of move and tell Bryson how she felt. The familiar paralysis had set in. Acknowledging her truth, she exited the contact list on her phone and sighed heavily.

ଓ

Bryson's cell phone rang. He looked at his hands-free monitor to view the name of the incoming caller and saw it was his sister Tara.

"Hey Sis!" he said after pressing the answer button.

"Hello brother!" Tara stated, "What are you up to?"

"I had an early dinner with Alton and have been running a few errands before going home. Mom and Dad have Duane, so I don't have to rush."

"Oh, so no date tonight?" Tara inquired.

"No, not tonight!" He stated. "I am probably going to spend some time in the studio and maybe watch movies."

"You know you can always come over, if you like," Tara offered. "If you don't want to be alone tonight..."

He knew this was her way of keeping up with his personal life. She was his older, slightly over-protective sister, but she was also his champion and true confidante. His mom knew him well, but it was Tara he could always talk to. She never betrayed his trust and came to his rescue whenever needed. She often warned him whenever she felt he was stepping into a place of concern. And although he had not always heeded her warnings or taken her advice, Tara never deserted him. Without her, his life with Duane would have been so much more arduous. 'Auntie Tara' was like a second mother to Duane, and he adored her. This warmed Bryson's heart, and he appreciated his sister more than words could convey, but he didn't need a check-in with her tonight. He had told her about his first date with Adria and she listened to his updates about their subsequent outings. She had mentioned the decrease in conversation about Adria the last time they spoke, but Bryson wasn't ready to talk to her about it—then or now.

"I think I am good, Sis!" Bryson responded.

"Well, we look forward to seeing you tomorrow at our Sunday feast," Tara shared. "Take care, love you!"

"Love you, too, Sis," Bryson stated, "Ciao!" And he hung up.

Bryson glanced at the clock on his radio as he continued his drive. He mentioned to Alton during dinner he had a song he wanted Adria to learn as a lead vocalist. As the evening was still young, he wondered if this would be a good time—and reason enough—to call Adria and check in. He only hesitated for a few minutes before he decided it was a good idea to give her a call.

Bryson drove into the nearby grocery store parking lot and pulled into an empty space. He then picked up his phone and located Adria's number and pressed the call button. The phone rang a couple of times before he heard Adria's voice exclaim, "Hello Bryson. What are you up to?"

"Hello, Sunshine!" Bryson responded cheerfully ... almost too cheerfully. He turned his tone down a notch. "Running a few errands. What are you doing? How was your dinner?" he asked politely, fighting the urge to allow his envy to resurface as he spoke with Adria. He knew he had no right to feel anything and tried to contain this unusual reaction to seeing Douglas and Adria together at the restaurant earlier. Most importantly, he understood this resentful response was not his usual behavior and it unnerved him.

"Dinner was good. Douglas is always fun to talk to!"

"I am glad you enjoyed your dinner. So, do you have any plans for the rest of the evening?" Bryson asked promptly.

"No, I am probably just going to watch a movie."

"Well, I'd like to see you," Bryson continued, then quickly added, "I have a song I want you to begin learning prior to the next lead vocalist's rehearsal."

"Okay," Adria responded, "I will be here."

"I need to make one more stop so why don't I drop by in an hour?" Bryson stated.

"Cool, I'll see you then."

"Ciao."

Bryson hung up and exited the parking lot to visit the Friendly Florist shop. He never visited her without bringing her favorite flower, a rose. Bryson reminded himself this was not a date, and he really did not need to bring her flowers, but this was his usual action. Adria adored roses and he enjoyed bringing them to her.

As he accelerated and checked his blind spot to switch lanes, he embraced an excited feeling growing within him, causing him to turn up the music and join in with the artists as he sang loudly and uninhibitedly.

CB

Adria stared at her phone. She did not have the courage to make the call herself, but things worked out in her favor anyway as Bryson called her and wanted to come over.

First things first. She needed to get ready for Bryson's visit. She grabbed her purse, went out to her car, and motored out of her driveway. She drove to the nearby grocery store to pick up a couple of items for the evening. The two ate dinner earlier, so Adria only wanted to arrange a cheese and fruit tray for snacking and to make sure she had enough beverages on hand.

There was a sensation in the pit of her stomach which could only be described as nervous excitement. The feeling continued as she completed her errand and returned to her home to prepare for Bryson's visit. Although this face-to-face meeting did not happen how she and Douglas discussed, she was grateful and remained open-minded.

Adria finished assembling the fruit and cheese tray and positioned it on the glass top round sofa table. She then went to her bathroom to freshen up. After dressing, she looked at herself in the full-length mirror. Happy with her outfit chosen, a pink and gray ensemble, accented with matching jewelry, Adria gave herself a nod of approval and went to her living room to wait. It had been almost an hour since Bryson called her and she knew he would soon be standing at her front door. She tried to not focus on the nervousness in her stomach and looked down at her hands to see if they were sweaty or shaking.

The doorbell rang. Adria walked to the front door and opened it.

"Well, hello there," Adria stated with a big smile. "Come on in!"

"Hello, Adria," Bryson arrived with three beautiful roses, one red, yellow, and white, with elegantly, wrapped gold and white lace paper, satin ribbons, and a wonderful smile. "These are for you."

"Thank you! They are beautiful," Adria said, accepting the flowers. And when they hugged, it was electric. She invited Bryson in. He walked into the living room and relaxed in the recliner. He placed the folder with the printed music lyrics on the table beside of the fruit tray.

"Excuse me for a minute. I want to put these in water," Adria announced and then walked into the kitchen to locate a vase. She placed the roses in water on the dining room table.

"Would you like a beverage?" she asked Bryson. "I have flavored sparkling waters."

Bryson requested a lemon water and helped himself to the gorgeously presented fruit and cheese tray. Adria returned with their drinks and began chatting about the day's activities.

"Douglas always reminds me of so many of our teenage experiences, many of which I had forgotten about," she said, and wistfully added, "A lot has happened since those days."

Adria recounted some of the stories, noting how intently Bryson listened to her. After a while of talking, she became silent and looked down at her water. She then quickly returned her attention to Bryson.

"Did you enjoy your dinner with Alton?"

"Yes, everything was great."

ଔ

Bryson reached over to pick up the folder with the music lyrics. He was ready to talk about the song and change the subject.

"I was really surprised when you and Alton walked in," Adria continued.

"Good surprise or bad surprise?" He looked into her eyes as he asked the question.

Adria looked down at her water again.

"Good surprise," she said quietly.

Bryson reminded himself again to focus on the music. But there was a mood in the air challenging him to move in a slightly different direction.

Bryson chuckled to himself and took another swallow of his beverage as he gazed at her face. "It had been a while since you and I hung out together. I guess we both have been a little busier than usual lately," he indicated.

"Yes, work has been hectic ... but," Adria said, then stopped, "Or rather and..."

Bryson looked over at Adria and waited silently for her to finish the sentence. He noticed she seemed a little nervous and was wondering what exactly was on her mind. Was she going to tell him she didn't want them to see each other again?

Bryson had gotten into his head and his mental energy was working overtime.

Then Adria started talking again.

"I know I have been kind of standoffish lately."

Bryson silently nodded his head in agreement. He prepared himself to focus on the song he wanted her to sing but allowed her to continue with her story.

"When I saw you for the very first time at GFCC, I thought you were incredible, and I admired your talents and your personality. When I found out you were single, I prayed and asked God to allow us to hang out for a while and if something could come out of it then so be it."

She took a swallow of her water.

"Then, I joined the choir, and we were together a lot..." Adria looked up into Bryson's eyes briefly before re-focusing her attention on the painting in front of her. She remained thoughtful. "When just the two of us went out a few times ... I don't know, it was like magic, and I was thrilled. Each time was cool. You made me laugh and I love to laugh."

ೞ

Adria noticed Bryson had leaned over the recliner's arm to listen more intently to her words. She now had Bryson's undivided attention.

"I guess I sort of got a little scared that I was feeling things which were one-sided."

"What do you mean?" Bryson asked quickly.

"I was falling for you, but I could not tell how you felt about me, so I backed off to make sure I didn't get hurt."

Adria had become very uncomfortable but desired the freedom that comes from being honest. And when she glanced at Bryson, he was nodding and attentive.

"Did you think I was seeing someone else?" He asked politely.

The ice was finally broken, and her courage increased. She could relax a little more now as she shared her truth.

"I knew we were both hanging out with different folks. So yeah, I was wondering if you met someone you were getting extra close to," Adria admitted, "and were not sure *how* to tell me. I do know there are a couple of ladies who are really head over heels in love with you and well, people do talk." Adria ended the conversation by shrugging her shoulders, glaring her eyes, and quickly lifting her eyebrows to her hairline.

Bryson laughed loudly.

"I have had a couple of girls trying to get extremely close. But if it had not been for the Lord on my side," Bryson laughed again, "I would have been in big trouble, so many times. Thank God for the Holy Ghost telling me when to stop!"

Adria laughed with him. "Good men, who are not mean-spirited and are smart, talented, and good looking are a novelty. Women are at a disadvantage. There are just not enough good men to go around, and we fight over you. Sometimes, it's simply about who can win. It sounds crazy, but it's true. You are a good man, Bryson, and I wasn't sure if I could handle the competition."

"What competition? You're the only one I've been thinking about," he responded honestly. "And I'll admit seeing you with Douglas today didn't set too well with me!"

"Really?" Adria responded immediately and allowed Bryson to continue to talk. "He and I have been friends a long time."

"Yes, I know, you told me that, but today you looked happy together in the restaurant. And I was upset because I have spent all of this time trying to get a handle on my feelings instead of just sharing my feelings," Bryson admitted quickly and then asked, "May I join you on the couch?"

"Sure." Adria patted the sofa cushions and leaned back onto the overstuffed couch for support. Bryson left the sanctity of the recliner and joined Adria. He sat at the opposite end to provide the distance for a safe atmosphere. Then he continued talking.

"There is a lot of pressure on men to make the right choices. It's not hard to be dogs and some ladies make it easy when they fight over us. It's like the minute one takes notice, then the other ten others stampede us. Then the phone calls and other gestures increase tremendously. As men, we love the attention, but we also have to deal with the issues this type of attention brings us and what you don't realize is when one of you steals our heart, actually gets into our heart, then we are hooked and it's not about anyone else." Bryson interlocked his hands to emphasize his point. "The tricky part is what it takes to get into our hearts and for every man it can be different—and it is not easy." He sighed before continuing. "For me, she has to

Adria's Transformation

be God-fearing, kind and beautiful; talented and family oriented; adventurous and open to things and smart!"

Adria stared with a look of astonishment at Bryson and asked pointedly, "What woman has mastered all of those characteristics?"

"You have all of those qualities and more, Adria, and I am just mesmerized."

Adria smiled bashfully and said softly, "Thank you." The compliment took her off guard and she could not conceal her embarrassment.

"Okay," Bryson then moved towards Adria, placed his arm around her waist and pulled her towards him. "Can we stop this charade and talk even more openly, because this is the moment of truth for me, and I am prepared to live in my truth."

"Yes," Adria responded quietly.

03

Bryson held her hand and looked into her eyes. Adria returned the gaze and looked back into his eyes as he slowly lowered his head to her face.

The next question Bryson wanted to ask never left his mouth as they both leaned in to enjoy their first kiss in weeks. When his face was close enough for their lips to touch, Adria closed her eyes, wanting to feel the warmth and the magic of the moment just before their lips actually met. She could still see his face through barely opened eyelids and could smell the scent of the breath mint he must have just put in his mouth previously without her knowledge.

Adria allowed herself to fully engage and enjoy the passionate, non-hurried kiss. She leaned into Bryson, and he pulled her even closer into a tight embrace. His soft full lips and her soft full lips were a perfect match.

In addition, there were a series of sweet, tender kisses and at the end of each they smiled but did not talk. Eventually, they hugged and leaned back on the couch to sit closely side by side, finally reconnected.

Adria placed her head on his shoulder and Bryson whispered in her ear, "I've missed you." She echoed the same words. The moment was tender and honest as they both relaxed together.

Adria felt the tears rolling down her face and they pulled apart. She rose to go to the kitchen to freshen up and Bryson followed her. They shared another quick kiss and Adria gave into the full-blown standing hug she wanted. The hug was healing and seemed to last forever!

At the end of the hug, they were standing close, leaning against the granite counter and Adria opened her mouth.

"I love you, Bryson."

Bryson did not miss a beat and declared, "I love you, Adria."

The hug continued a while longer before they walked hand and hand back into the living room. The couple returned to sit closely on the sofa and continued their socializing.

Within one hour and a half, the atmosphere in Adria's home had drastically changed. They were in a good place and the stress level had tremendously decreased. Music played in the background and assisted with creating the optimal atmosphere. Although Adria was relaxing and enjoying the music, she felt compelled to speak first and break the silence.

"You know, I don't think either of us were hiding our feelings for each other very well," Adria admitted as she looked at Bryson.

"So, I have been told. I am glad we are at this point. It feels like a major weight has been lifted off my shoulders!"

Adria reflected silently on the fact that true love wasn't something that could be hidden, it was palpable, showing up in the room before anyone uttered a sound. It could be felt. Understanding that, Adria admitted silently she had been fighting these feelings because she did not want to be wrong about their interactions.

Bryson made himself more comfortable, then reached for Adria's hand for a reconnection. To her, their hands together felt like a perfect fit. The mood remained peaceful.

"Does this mean we are dating exclusively?" Bryson asked boldly. He was looking at her face so as not to seemingly miss her immediate reaction.

"Yes, I think this is exactly what it means," Adria confessed and then asked, "Do you think our parents will be happy we are together?"

"My life is a little more complicated because I have Duane. I am not sure how your folks are going to accept this reality. Just be ready, as there are a few people who will be in shock we are a couple."

Adria looked at Bryson as he spoke.

"Well, the two of us are the adults who really matter in this scenario. We will have to stick together when people try to pull us apart."

Adria then repositioned herself at the left end of the sofa and placed a pillow in her lap and signaled for

Bryson to join her. He then stretched out on his side and laid his head on the pillow.

Adria looked down at the restful face of her new boyfriend and spoke.

"You know, Bryson, you have an incredible calling on your life and God wants to really use you. Your music ministry is outstanding and every time I hear you exalt in our concerts and between songs; I can feel the anointing in your voice."

Bryson glanced up at Adria's face and chuckled.

"Your calling is also extremely visible. You can hear it when you sing. I guess we both need to stop running away from what God has in store for both of us!"

Adria sighed.

"In the past I have not wanted to embrace any type of calling. It all seemed unreachable and unattainable for me. I became bitter and angry. I was too broken to do anything. That was the excuse I had been using. I didn't always nurture it like I should." Adria confessed. "From my standpoint Christians in my church were so cold-hearted, mean, and forceful. And they had no balance in their lives. Many of them never really seemed happy, except knowing they were going to live in eternity with God. But their day to day lives were in shambles. It caused me to have so many questions and I pulled away from God. But He was merciful, patient and kind and waited for me to get my act together."

"So, you can have a testimony!" Bryson exclaimed, sitting up. "The world needs to see how God can pick us up out of anything and use us despite of our shortcomings. Lord knows, I am not perfect Adria, far from it, but I love God and I know He loves me back."

Bryson paused, and then with a little hesitancy, asked, "Is that really why you left the church and this town?"

"There was a lot going on with me then. It was pretty complicated," Adria responded and offered no further explanation. When she offered no more, he laid back down. Adria began to rub his arm lightly with her fingers as they continued to talk.

"In the past, a night like this probably would have gone a little differently for me," Bryson admitted. "But I am not focused on that right now. It is the spiritual connection you and I have that makes me want us to be different."

Adria raised her eyebrows and made a facial reaction that agreed with Bryson.

"I just know our conversations are really deep. To me, the physical activity is always the easy part, but the deep spiritual connection is now my top priority. Let's keep it real, though, it can become tricky at times," Adria added. "One very good kiss, or a lot of great kisses, can turn this into a sexual interaction in just a few minutes!"

"True," Bryson agreed, "But I am at the time in my life where I want," he paused briefly, "no, where I require much more than the physical connection."

Adria felt more and more at home with Bryson and was happy they were one at this point tonight.

"This is amazing," Adria thought silently. This was the type of moment she desired, as it was different from her past relationships. She hoped this could grow into something much, much more.

സ

In the middle of this moment of sharing Bryson began to hear a song melody in his head. It was just a couple of chords, followed by words. Instinctively, he began to hum the same tune repeatedly.

"What are you singing?" Adria inquired.

"It's something new that's popping up in my head. I am getting inspired. Let's go to the keyboard for a second. Can I borrow a pen and some paper?" he asked sitting up again.

Bryson excused himself to go to the restroom before meeting Adria in the study/music area where she kept the keyboard she used to practice her singing. She had a strong ear for music but mostly preferred to pick up chord structures on her own. Adria offered Bryson a pad of paper and a pen and gave him space to play the song he heard in his heart. He stopped long enough to write down some lyrics and musical notations.

Adria sat in the chair beside the keyboard and watched him lovingly as he worked. He was intense and every now and then would stop and wink at her. The chord structures were jagged at first, but slowly they began to take on a more harmonic arrangement.

When she stood up to use the restroom, he touched her hand and declared, "You can't go anywhere just yet, you're my inspiration."

"Your inspiration has to go to the bathroom."

With that response Adria excused herself and Bryson returned to the song creation process. When Adria returned, Bryson sang a few lines of the song and shared with her his thoughts and ideas before he asked her to join in. It felt like a soloist's rehearsal session when he instructed her on how to sing notes and allow her voice to flow through the lyrics. But this was a different

Adria's Transformation

interaction between them. Sharing the song tonight had a very special meaning because of their feelings.

Eventually, Bryson stopped and said, "Hey sweetie, I am just zoning right now and really need the equipment in my home studio. The music in my head just won't stop flowing."

"No problem. I will never stand in the way of creativity."

"I appreciate it," Bryson added, "You are stuck with me now!"

Bryson gathered up his things and Adria walked him to the front door. He stopped just before the door was opened to give her another kiss and hug before saying, "'What a wonderful day! Can't wait to see you tomorrow!"

Adria blew him a kiss once he was inside of his car. She watched her man back out of the driveway and accelerate down the street. When she returned into the inside of the house, she threw her hands up in the air and shouted, "Thank you, thank you, thank you, God! You are awesome!"

Then she danced around the living room, into the kitchen, and into the bedroom. She finished her nightly chores while humming the melody to the new song she and Bryson were just working on.

Adria could not remember a time when she was this elated. God had smiled on her once again. When she thought about how much He had blessed her in the past few years, her eyes watered. In addition to all the things He had already done, God had given her a prince, a warrior, a minister.

She continued her joviality until she was tired and exhausted. The last thing she remembered as she snuggled in her bed and after her prayers was the way it felt to kiss Bryson and to have his arms around her in a wonderful hug.

༄

Bryson drove home as fast as he could to finish his song. He didn't have time to be distracted by the day's activities as he knew the song would capture them most eloquently. He spent the twenty-minute drive humming the tune and reciting the words into the audio recorder on his phone. He explored vocal modulations and different keys. He was having fun with the new song and was thankful for the inspiration.

Bryson turned into his driveway parked his car in his garage and moved quickly into his home to begin working on his passion.

In his music studio, Bryson was truly at ease. He could be creative, totally free and allow God to direct his path. Here he could express in music what he cannot always express verbally.

Throughout the song development process, he thought of Adria and became even more inspired. The song needed a base scripture, so he turned to the books of Psalm/Proverbs for further guidance. When he was utterly exhausted, he glanced at the clock. It indicated he had been in the zone for two hours or more. During this time, musical tracks had been captured. Not all of the lyrics were audible at this point, but he knew words would flow in the future as before. At this point, though, he needed rest.

Bryson walked to his bedroom and prepared himself for sleep. Before he drifted into slumber mode and after his prayers, he thought of Adria, of her kisses and the way she fit perfectly in his arms when they hugged. Audibly he stated, "God, you are so good!" and then settled down for his time of calm sleep.

Dr. Paula Y. Obie

Chapter 4
Sunday Blessings

Adria had never been a morning person, so it took a while for all the senses to connect, and she became a "whole" being. On this morning, however, she did not perform the ritual of pressing the 'snooze' button at least three or four times, as her usual routine called for. Instead, she let her alarms draw her out of sleep. She rolled over to look out the window. The sun seemed unusually bright this morning and she felt warm and loved!

Adria closed her eyes and focused on the word 'loved.' She was loved! She smiled as she thought not only of God's love for her, but also Bryson's, which he had vocalized the previous evening. She opened her eyes and sat up in the bed.

"But wait, what day is this?" Adria asked herself silently. It occurred to her it was Sunday morning! She moved quickly out of the bed to get ready. She started singing as she marched into the kitchen for the morning cup of coffee and turned on the radio.

The Saints in Praise were singing, *"This is the day that the Lord has made, and I will rejoice and be glad in it."* It was the Sabbath, and she was ready to give God some praise.

Adria arrived at GFCC at 10:40 a.m. and took her seat in the sanctuary. The service started with the Praise & Worship team ushering in the Holy Spirit at 10:45 a.m. and by 11:10 a.m., the church atmosphere had caught on fire. No one wanted the praise to end. Bishop joined in with the praise. The church ministers' arms were in the air as they took their perspective places. It was a Holy Ghost party.

When Adria glanced at the clock at 11:30 a.m., the atmosphere had calmed down enough for the order of service to be adhered to. The Minister in Charge tried hard to restore order but whenever a series of "Hallelujahs," or "Thank You, Jesus," or "Glory!" would erupt, there would begin another chorus of praise and dancing in the spirit.

Adria looked to the musician's corner, where Bryson sat during service. He had sweat rolling down his face, while the musicians were animated and being blessed by God's presence as it filled the church. They were smiling and looking around, taking in the joyousness of the morning. At key times, Bryson would reach over and grab his towel to wipe his face as he directed the musicians into the next round of musical activity.

The Minister in Charge announced the person who would deliver the morning invocation and read the scripture before the choir, Youth 'n Praise, an energetic teenage chorus who practiced diligently to deliver God's music from a young person's point of view, provided their opening selection. The initial song was powerful, and spirit filled. The whole church was on their feet before the lead vocalist could finish the first verse.

"This must be what heaven would be like all the time," thought Adria. She closed her eyes and allowed herself to soak in the atmosphere. Her eyes filled with tears which rolled down both cheeks as Bishop reminded the congregation that even during troubled times there were so many things to be thankful for. She was so grateful for the power of God in the sanctuary this morning.

Adria looked again at the musician's corner. Bryson had finally given into his exhaustion and allowed the second shift musician to replace him at the Hammond organ. He moved into his chair and took a long swallow from the bottled water offered by the nursing staff.

Although he was exhausted, he took a moment to survey the sanctuary in praise. He seemed to be searching for someone, and when their eyes met, he smiled. Then he made a face and blew outward indicating how hard he had worked. She, in turn, nodded her head, in understanding. Their interaction was tender and innocent and only interrupted when Bishop prepared to speak.

Adria listened attentively to the message and appreciated how Bishop allowed the atmosphere of worship to flow freely. He challenged everyone in attendance to find gratitude in their everyday situations, especially when faced with something difficult and called the elders to the altar for intercessory prayer. Then the invitational song began. It was an original composition by Bryson that encouraged its listeners on how to give everything to the Lord. The entire congregation joined in with the chorus as folks moved to the prayer warriors for the intercessory prayer time.

Slowly
If you have problems, you cannot solve, (Just).
Take them to the altar and leave them there! (repeat)

Give it to Jesus, (Repeat x5)
He's waiting at the alter with open arms, With Him you are not alone!
Just Give it to Jesus and leave it there.
(Oh, Oh, Oh, Oh, Oh) unison, Repeat (harmony)

As Bishop and the Elders attended to those needing prayer, the choir sang a second song which was a little bit more upbeat. The service ended on a high note, and attendees left the worship experience greeting and hugging their neighbors.

Adria walked past First Lady Becca and gave her a hug. Normally they talked only for a few minutes, but today she held onto her arm, signaling for her to remain close. Adria moved to the side pew and gave her ample time to greet the rest of the members and guests.

Adria greatly admired First Lady Becca and felt she was the epitome of a true Bishop's wife. She was humble and holy, and loved God, her husband, and her family. She also was a minister and the overseer of the women's ministries at GFCC. Her ability to reach both the young and the older women in the church was grounded in her love for people.

Adria watched how she offered her greetings, without skipping anyone. She waved her hands to the many folks she could not physically hug or touch. First Lady Becca could be considered a shy person, but she was a fireball when given the opportunity to speak. When her hands positioned themselves around a microphone she transformed. After she completed her greetings, she placed her full attention on Adria.

"Wow, don't you look great this morning! How are you doing, sweetie?" the First Lady exclaimed.

Adria's Transformation

"Thank you, I am doing fine. I enjoyed this morning's service."

"It was awesome. And so was the 7:45 a.m. service. This Sunday was a time God truly decided to just show up and hang out with us all day. And I have praised up on an appetite. Do you have plans for lunch?"

"No ma'am, I don't have any plans at the moment. I am just still in awe of what I witnessed this morning." Adria answered.

"How would you like to join the Bishop and me for lunch?" First Lady Becca asked and gave Adria a warm smile as she gathered her belongings.

"Sure, I'd love to," Adria responded and tried not to appear shocked at the invitation, although in truth, her heart was racing, and her stomach felt a little uneasy. This was the first time she had been invited to lunch with them.

"Wonderful!"

First Lady Becca placed her hand on top of Adria's and guided her to the pastoral study area, where the Bishop and the others gathered. Adria remained in shock and failed to send Bryson a text with this news. But she felt her phone vibrate as soon as she and First Lady Becca turned the corner to enter the Offices of Administration and Pastoral Study. There, she saw Bryson walking towards them, his eyes on his phone—he was texting her.

First Lady Becca greeted him and took the time to offer compliments and words of encouragement. Bryson received her hugs and expressions of inspiration. He peered across First Lady's shoulders, saw Adria, and smiled broadly. Adria returned a big smile. She reached into her purse for the phone and glanced to see the text message from Bryson.

Bryson then greeted Adria.

"I was also invited to lunch," Adria responded, replying to the message he sent her.

First Lady Becca walked over to speak to her husband. "Do you have any idea where we are going to eat today, Bishop?"

As he contemplated where he wanted to have his luncheon, the pulpit ministers, the Minister in Charge and their spouses entered the Bishop's Suite. Bishop suggested the buffet at the Green's Café, and everyone agreed.

გე

Bryson looked at Adria and asked if she wanted to ride with him.

"Can we drop my car off at my house as it is on the way and then you won't have to come way back out here?"

"That works," Bryson stated, then he turned to the group and added, "Okay, Bishop, we'll meet you all there!" He placed his hand on Adria's back to guide her down the hall and out the doors to their cars.

Bryson followed Adria to her home and waited as she parked her car in the garage. He watched as Adria walked out of the garage towards his car and pressed the button on her key chain to close the garage doors. She slid into the passenger seat and placed her clutch and bag with the flat shoes in the back seat.

"How's my girl?" Bryson asked cheerfully.

"She's wonderful; and how's my guy?" Adria parroted.

"Fulfilled!"

"Good answer!"

Adria's Transformation

Then they leaned over to have their first quick Sunday kiss. Adria lovingly stroked Bryson's face with her right hand. He winked at her and placed the car in reverse to back out of the driveway to meet the Bishop, First Lady Becca and pulpit ministers and spouses. They listened to the morning's church service CD on their way to the restaurant. They talked a little, but mostly listened and reacted to the morning worship service.

"Whew, I absolutely loved this morning. It was incredible," Adria exclaimed.

Bryson nodded his head.

"It was powerful! From the musician's area it was almost as if there was a fog in the building. I was sweating profusely. This morning was one of the few mornings I wanted to just stop playing and start my own praise party."

"I guess it's not fair to the musicians. I think we worked you all extra hard today!"

Bryson laughed, then said, "Well, we're here! Let's go show some love!" He parked the car, opened his door, and walked around to Adria's side and then opened the passenger door to help her out of the car.

As they walked towards the restaurant, they could see Bishop and First Lady along with the ministers walking through the door, so their timing was on point.

"Does any of the other musicians get invited to lunch with the Bishop after Sunday service?" Adria asked him.

"Sometimes," Bryson responded quickly and offered no other explanation as he focused his attention opening the door for her and joining the others. He resisted the urge to hold Adria's hand, thinking it might be too soon to announce their new relationship to everyone and stated, "Lunch is on me today—if Bishop decides to let someone else pay the bill."

Adria smiled, "Sounds good to me."

☙

After the lunch, Bishop and First Lady lingered around Bryson and Adria for a few extra moments. To Adria, it was not totally obvious, but it appeared they personally wanted to show extra love to the new couple. Their hugs and words of encouragement were earnest; and with that, Adria felt God had placed His stamp of approval on the relationship.

They departed from the Bishop and First Lady, and Adria and Bryson walked to the car and prepared to drive out of the parking lot. Several church associates and church board members had been in attendance at the restaurant. One of the board members now walked over to Bryson.

"Hello Minister Bryson! Who is this beautiful lady you have with you?" She asked.

Bryson introduced Adria. They chatted for a few minutes and all-in-all, it was a pleasant interaction, but it confirmed to Adria that others were also watching.

Once they said their goodbyes and Bryson and Adria drove out of the restaurant parking lot, Bryson was the first to speak.

"That went well," Bryson said. "I mean with Bishop and First Lady."

"Yes, very well. I felt like they both breathed a sigh of relief that you and I were hanging out together," Adria shared as she looked forward.

Adria's Transformation

"Bishop and I talked briefly on last week and he had a lot of good things to say about you," Bryson said.

"About me? Really?" Adria asked surprised to hear she had been part of the conversation.

"Yes, he asked me frankly if you and I were dating and if we were serious," he said, matter-of-factly. "I told him we had gone out a few times and I hoped it could be more, but I really wasn't sure."

Adria became silent. She was shocked Bishop had discussed their relationship with Bryson. However, she should not have been surprised as he would be knowledgeable of who was associated with his Minister of Music. That was to be expected.

"It does feel good to be accepted by Bishop and First Lady. I sorta' felt they knew something. First Lady has always been cordial to me, but today, she was more like a mother figure," Adria stated.

Bryson reached out for her hand and brought it to his lips. "It's okay, baby; I approve of us too!" His quick wit removed the tension out of the conversation, helping Adria to feel warm and fuzzy on the inside. She stroked the side of Bryson's face. This had become one of her new favorite responses since they confessed their love for each other, and she took every opportunity to do so. "Now, tell me about your new song!" Adria exclaimed, as she changed the subject.

Bryson reported how the music unfolded from the night before and even sang a little bit of the song. Adria recognized the melody and some of the lyrics from the previous evening.

"I like it!" Adria nodded admirably and relaxed her head back on the headrest.

"Are you tired?" Bryson inquired.

"I am a little tired; and the truth is, if I go home, I will probably take a nap."

"Let's go to the park and walk around for a while," Bryson suggested.

Adria agreed and this was their next stop. Bryson parked the car and Adria removed her pumps and replaced them with her flat shoes. Bryson grabbed her hand, and they strolled leisurely around, walking and talking.

"What a difference a day makes," Adria stated. "Yesterday, I was in a totally different mindset."

"What kind of mindset?" Bryson inquired.

"My mind was filled with a lot of questions, and now I have many of them answered," Adria added. "My head is not so cluttered."

Bryson's response was to place his arms around her waist to hold her closer. As they strolled through the paths, they chuckled at the small children running around and enjoying life.

"What are your thoughts about having children?" Bryson asked, as he turned to watch the kids run around and tumble on the ground. One of them began to cry loudly and the parents were attentive and came to his rescue.

"I actually love children and always envisioned I'd have a house full of them like my Mom and Dad. Now that I'm older, I realize I don't necessarily need a house full, but just a couple to make my life complete," Adria announced, then asked. "How is Duane doing these days?"

"Duane is wonderful. He is growing so fast and it's hard to believe he is four years old! I love having him with

Adria's Transformation

me on weekends, though on this Sunday, he is spending time with his grandparents," Bryson reflected.

"He is such a cutie and looks a lot like his father," Adria acknowledged and then looked over at Bryson's face. He gave her an appreciative smile but continued talking.

"So last night was a big turning point for us, Adria," Bryson confessed, "I mean, we are still getting to know each other but I really want for us to do this right. I had this feeling of gratitude when I woke up this morning simply because of us and I don't want to mess that up."

Adria saw the sincerity in his eyes and couldn't help the warm and fuzzy feelings that had filled her heart again.

"I agree," Adria responded.

Bryson reached over and grabbed her hand.

"Are you ready to head back?"

The couple turned around and walked to the car and exited the park.

"Is there any other place you'd like to go?" Bryson asked as he eased his car into traffic.

"You're the driver, I am just enjoying my day," Adria said and when Bryson didn't reply immediately, she added, "We could always go and watch movies at my place if you want to come and hang out."

"Okay, cool. Let's do that, then I can relax a bit."

Soon, Adria and Bryson arrived at her home and prepared to unwind. They decided to watch one of her favorite films and one of his. And then got comfortable. Bryson grabbed a blanket and sat in the recliner, while Adria removed a cover from the back of the sofa.

"Times have truly changed," Adria laughed as she positioned herself in a comfortable place.

"In what way?" Bryson asked as he yawed loudly.

"Growing up, we were never allowed to go to the movies," Adria explained, "And now, I get to watch as many movies at home as I want to *and* go to the movie theater if I like."

"Yes, the Darden and Kenton families have come a long way from our early childhood, haven't we?" Bryson added with another audible yawn.

"Absolutely!" Adria agreed as she settled even more comfortably on her sofa and pillow and began watching the first film. Once the second movie started, both of them fell asleep. At one point, Adria awoke, peered over at Bryson, and reminded herself they were now truly a couple. She thought about the luncheon with Bishop, First Lady, and the other attendees. Then she thought about the church board member and pondered briefly if she was prepared for the type of visibility she was about to receive. She forced the thought from her mind, snuggled under the blanket, closed her eyes, and fell back into her afternoon slumber.

Chapter 5
You Need To Know The Truth

"So, when were *you* going to tell me you and Bryson were dating seriously? I heard it from one of the GFCC women's ministry leaders," Adria's younger sister, Francine, asked, as they talked on the phone. She was three years younger than Adria and the youngest offspring in the Darden family. Francine was not the easiest person to get along with particularly if she felt she was the last person to know something, and because of that, she tended to come off as extremely judgmental, often jumping to a lot of wrong or exaggerated conclusions.

"You knew we were going out. We've been hanging out for months now," Adria answered.

"Hanging out with the chorale group and going out every now and then, yes, but from what I hear, you are now in love?" Francine asked with an air of sarcasm.

The sisters spoke regularly, with Francine sharing many of the home scenarios Adria missed out on; but also, Francine bringing up her drastic decision to move to another state and limiting her communication with the family for an entire decade. Adria knew her younger sister staying in Rockville affected her view on the matter, but she also understood Francine was lashing out from the hurt she felt when Adria walked away from the family right after she graduated from college. Francine felt the pain of rejection, for which Adria was the cause. For that reason, even though Adria's therapist, Dr. Bailey, advised her more than once to not allow herself to be addicted to Francine's toxicity, she continued the weekly phone chats with Francine. Adria had abandoned her baby sister once, and she did not want to abandon or reject her sister again.

"Uhm, yes ... we are in love, but truthfully Francine, we have been in love for a while and now we are being real and are no longer hiding it," Adria shared as she tried to remain calm. She focused on her excitement about falling in love with Bryson, even as she understood their relationship may not be accepted by members of her family, especially Mama Darden.

"Hiding it why?" Francine inquired. "Did you find out about the other girlfriends he keeps on speed dial?"

Adria rolled her eyes.

"I don't know anything about any girlfriends, but he is pretty high profiled," Adria commented. She wanted to end the phone call, but because this was a topic Douglas also brought up, Adria continued listening.

"Yep, and from what I understood he has slept with every woman in the church! As a matter of fact, there is some girl who says she is pregnant, and he is the father!" Francine shared.

Adria felt flustered.

"Maybe that was why I chose to keep my feelings hidden for a while. First, to make sure it was not just lust or a strong attraction—"

"Which is probably what it really is," Francine interjected.

"I also wanted to watch his life, to really get to know him—"

"How can you truthfully watch his life?" Francine cut in again. "Some guys are really, really good at hiding things, especially another girlfriend or spouse. We see it on documentaries all the time."

"I have made it a point to observe his life for the past eight months, Francine," Adria added, "I mean, we are in the same place a lot. We are in weekly choir rehearsals, lead vocalists' rehearsals, choir renderings and the choir social dinners and lunches held after we sing. I have not seen anything but a God-fearing, Black man. I mean, of course, I was curious if he was seeing anyone when we first started hanging out, and like ADULTS, we talked about it."

"Just keep on looking, Sis, and make sure you are *not* in denial," Francine advised. "And remember, you have not dated him for the entire eight months. You don't really know what he was doing when you were not around. Don't be naïve, you know how you are! You always overlook the obvious!"

Adria ignored Francine's last sentence before continuing. There was a time when Adria trusted the wrong people and they took advantage of her kindness. However, those times were in her *past*, where they belonged.

"You sound as if you personally have had an experience with him. Have the two of you slept together and I just missed it?"

Francine was silent for a few seconds.

"No... but I know a couple of girls who he's been with, and they do not speak very highly of him."

"Why did they break up?" Adria probed.

"Women ... he is women crazy. He can't have just one. One of the girls is a good friend of mine, Mary, and she really went through it. He treated her like dirt. She would do anything in the world for him, even now, and he never appreciated her. She was so crazy about him, I thought she was going to commit suicide when they stopped seeing each other. We had to really pray for her."

Adria was appalled and shocked at her sister's stories. The man Francine described was not the Bryson she knew. Her sister was known to exaggerate and be dramatic, so Adria was careful to not hang onto her every word. However, she also knew there had to be some level of truth to the accusations being leveled against Bryson. She wondered what percentage that could be.

"How do you know all of this, Francine?" Adria asked calmly.

"Everybody knows this, Adria!" Francine answered. Everybody!"

Adria could feel herself growing agitated, but she decided to calm her emotions and get to the bottom of this.

"Why was he allowed to be a Minister of Music if he had this reputation?" she challenged.

"Because he is great at what he does," Francine responded. "I mean you can't deny the boy is talented. And the music department improved one hundred

Adria's Transformation

percent when he took over. It caused the membership to rise, and more members equals higher offerings!"

"How long has he been at GFCC?" Adria continued.

"About three years, I think."

If Bryson had only been at GFCC for about three years, then maybe he had not had time to be with *every* woman in the congregation, although she understood it was enough time to develop a bad reputation, she noted silently.

What was she thinking, listening to her sister like this?! Even though her guilt was ever present, Adria understood she couldn't continue to pander to her sister's anger. And that's all this was. It was more visible at certain times than others; today, her sister was extremely vocal.

"I am just *not* familiar with the person you described. And you know just how women can be, especially a woman scorned," Adria declared, "We have seen first-hand with our own brothers, how situations can become crazy in a short amount of time."

"I'm just telling you the truth."

Adria's heart became heavy. This was supposed to be a time of celebration for her. Yet, here she was, fielding accusations being lobbed against Bryson. She loved him dearly and the last thing she wanted to hear was this type of story about him from Francine. And while she knew that she should trust what she knew about Bryson, the truth was she didn't know him all that well. Her mind raced as she desperately needed to know how much of what Francine was saying was true or false.

"Well, I think I've heard enough Francine." said Adria, with a nervous chuckle, "I am going to go now. Talk to you later."

Adria pressed the End button on the cordless phone before Francine had the chance to say anything else and dropped her head.

"Why is it that when you find a man who you think is perfect for you in so many ways you find out he is promiscuous, or gay, or a drug addict, or a liar, or a thief or whatever," she pondered silently. "And a Christian man, on top of all that!"

As much as she wanted to, Adria could not ignore what she had heard. Good or bad, right or wrong, she had to find out if any of it was true, or if it was, as Bryson said, just the cost that came with being in the position he was in.

Silently, she pondered, how would Bryson find the time to be with so many women? Was she in denial about his true character? On the other hand, she just could not see Bishop allowing him to have this type of bad reputation as the Minister of Music at GFCC.

However, like Francine stated, the Music Department had made major improvements and impacted the church's growth. Maybe the Bishop and the Board Members were willing to overlook his indiscretions because of this reality.

Adria participated in the Women's Bible study group, and the choir, but otherwise, she did not engage in numerous conversations with a lot of women at the church. What she perceived was many women *wanted* him, but she thought he was picky and only dated a certain type of lady.

Adria thought about the instances when Diane, a fellow soprano, hovered over him frequently. It was not news how Diane would get extra close to Bryson as this was something she did quite often. She was a very pretty girl who used her femininity to get what she wants from men, but she had also witnessed how Bryson worked hard to keep her at a distance.

And after she joined GFCC, most of the time Bryson and Adria co-mingled in the large group setting and the atmosphere was casual. It didn't present an opportunity for people to gossip about them being in the same place at the same time.

Surely all that meant Bryson wasn't the person Francine said he was. So why did these stories persist?

"What am I going to do, Lord?" Adria asked verbally.

Adria realized she was thinking way too hard and decided to go for a walk. It only took a few minutes to change into the walking shoes, grab a bottled water and her keys. She opened the front door and strolled out into a sunny day with a slight breeze.

Adria walked along the sidewalk in her neighborhood. She power-walked for a significant distance before she felt the tension from the phone call slowly dissipate from her body. Her thoughts were not racing like before and her emotions were within a more normal range.

At one point she felt her eyes begin to water, but she commanded herself not to cry as she needed to first learn the whole truth. Right now, all she could do was hope the report was mostly gossip and not be judgmental if even a percentage of it was true. She was certainly not a perfect person and had depended on God to mature her to this point.

Bryson didn't even know everything about her past. She had only told him a small part of her story as to why she moved away from her family suddenly and stayed away from the church. But she also had not shared a great amount of detail of her life during her time away. How dare she be angry about accusations which have not been validated prior to the time when they began dating?

What if he were in her shoes and had to confront some of the stories about her behavior within the past decade, delivered to him by a family member and friend? Would he give her grace?

"Why was it we want others to be perfect, but we required lots of mercy for ourselves?" Adria thought as she reached the end of the residential area and made a U-turn to head back in the direction of her house.

Yes, she would face these issues—about Bryson and about sharing her own story—but only when the timing was right. Maybe this was all nothing.

How would she respond though if it turned out that Bryson had been with more than one woman at GFCC? Would those women come up to her and tell her they had slept with Bryson? Lord, have mercy! And if this behavior was in his past, what impact should it have on their relationship now?

Completely flustered, Adria returned home to hear her home phone ringing. She wasn't able to get to it in time and missed the call. She checked her home voice mail system when she saw the red light blinked.

'Hi sweetie, I am thinking about you and wanted to give you a call. Give me a ring when you get a chance ... I love you!'

She checked her phone voice mail, and the message was similar.

'Just called your home phone and you were not there. I guess you are out and about. Give me a call when you are free, I love you!'

Adria's Transformation

"His actions are sure *not* of a true womanizer," she thought, "I wonder what caused him to have this bad reputation?"

Even so, Adria didn't rush to call him back. She needed some space. The walk accomplished a lot of positive things for her physical, emotional, and mental well-being and rather than jump into something she felt she wasn't ready for, Adria took the time to shower and relax. She settled down with another bottled water to watch one of her favorite Hallmark movies. She did not get through the first commercial before her phone rang.

Annoyed by the interruption, she listened to the ring tone to confirm Bryson was the caller.

"Since when did he decide to become so persistent ... and why today?" she thought. She really needed her space now.

Adria reluctantly accepted the call, though, and placed the phone on speaker.

"Hello," she said, a little curtly.

"Well, hello, sunshine," Bryson stated enthusiastically.

"Hi, how are you?" Adria responded.

"Are you okay, you sound a little down in the dumps?" Bryson inquired.

"Yeah, had a bit of a rough morning, but I am good. I just returned from my walk and had my shower. I am getting ready to watch a movie."

"I am calling to ask you if you wanted to go out to see a movie. Alton and Val and two other couples were thinking about going to a matinee. I told Alton I'd check with you to see if you were up to it," Bryson added.

Adria cleared her throat before answering.

"What movie are you going to see?" Her level of enthusiasm remained low.

"We have not made a decision yet, but Alton and Val are great at choosing the best movies," Bryson said. "So, what do you think, do you want to join them?"

Adria thought about it for a moment and knew no good would come from her sitting at home stewing about the situation. Besides, it would give her a chance to hang out with a few folks to see if she noticed signs of the accusations Francine discussed earlier. She would listen to the women around her intently to see if they offered any insight at all into Bryson's character. Regardless of what she did or did not learn, Adria promised herself she would keep an open mind and not jump to any conclusions.

"Sure, why not."

"Great, then I'll pick you up shortly, say, within the hour. How does that sound?"

"Works for me!" Adria replied.

Adria continued to let the movie play on the TV while she prepared for Bryson's arrival. When she was satisfied with her outfit, she surveyed herself in the mirror and smiled gently knowing she looked pretty good; however, her mood remained somber, her suspicious and pessimistic nature now stirred.

೦ಙ

Bryson arrived as he promised in an hour. Adria opened the door and smiled gently.

As he entered the house, he leaned over and gave Adria a full kiss on the lips. When Bryson pulled away from her lips, he looked at her and noticed she was not wearing her usual radiant smile. It was as he had suspected: his new girlfriend was not herself today. She decided to go out with them though. He was sure she would be cheerful by the end of the night. He would see to it she was smiling within a few hours.

"Are you ready?" he asked.

"Yes, I am," Adria answered softly.

The two of them walked to the car and as was the usual custom, he opened the passenger door for her and waited until she was inside before walking around to the driver's side and into the seat.

As he clicked his seat belt, he glanced over at her and enquired, "Do you feel okay, sweetie?"

"I've been better. I hope going to the movies will help my disposition," Adria responded truthfully as she settled in her seat.

"Do you wanna talk about it?" he asked as he backed out of the driveway.

"Maybe sometime tonight, but not right now." Adria ended the sentence by looking at him and smiling slightly before also adding, "I'm okay."

Bryson knew enough about women to understand when to back off. A sweet little lamb chop could become a raging tigress if the aggravation continued. Especially after she had already stated she didn't want to talk. There was something that had Adria in this type of mood, but Bryson was going to have to trust they would communicate at some point.

○○

The other couples—Alton and Val, Jerome and Millicent, and Curtis and SueEllen—arrived at the movie theatre and after they spent time making the proper greetings, they prepared to go inside. The movie was scheduled to start in a few minutes, and the ladies found seats in the lobby and began to visit.

SueEllen directed her attention to Adria.

"Girl, you were some kinda sharp on the fourth Sunday. From head to toe, you looked like you just stepped out of a magazine. All of us were jealous," SueEllen admitted.

"I told Alton I had never seen you look so radiant and wondered what had changed," Val inquired and made a melodramatically cute face as she looked up into the ceiling, "Because you were positively glowing, and it made you look even more beautiful."

"Is this love, is this love, is this love, is this love that I'm feeling," teased Millicent as she sang the lyrics to a popular song.

Though Adria didn't respond, she could feel happiness beginning to work its magic on her. She was slowly starting to feel better. The ladies laughed as the men moved closer to their group.

"Well, is it?" Val asked again as she waited to get a response from Adria.

"It sure feels like it," Adria admitted shyly and smiled. When she finished the sentence, she wrinkled her nose and raised her shoulders up and down for emphasis. Her heart was still a little heavy, but at the same time, she knew her love for Bryson had been growing for quite a while. She was struggling emotionally and mentally.

"Girl, you wear it well and I wish you all the best." Millicent added.

Alton walked over and asked, "Ladies, are you ready?"

Adria's Transformation

Each lady then walked over to their prospective partners and proceeded into the movies. When they settled on a seat, Bryson asked Adria how she was feeling. She looked at his face to see his genuine concern and admitted she was feeling much better. Adria turned her body towards Bryson and grabbed a hold of his hand. She wasn't sure if it was for extra reassurance for him or her, but he welcomed her hand and held on tight.

At the end of the movie, the couples were ready to continue the fellowship and once the restaurant was finally decided on, made their way across town to their destination.

In the car, Bryson initiated the conversation with Adria.

"Did you enjoy the movie?" Bryson asked as they drove to the restaurant.

"Yes, I did. It was a little intense at times, but the points were well taken. The screenwriter did not mind making the hard points."

"No, he didn't. I was a little uncomfortable as I felt really badly for the girl. But in the end, she was able to get an even better man," Bryson declared cheerfully.

"It's hard to believe men can treat women that way, but it's true." Adria's voice drifted off.

Bryson glanced over at her.

"There are still some good men out here. All of us are not cruel."

"No, but a lot of you *are* and to be fair some of it is our fault. A lot of women are not very nice, and they just run the man away. And sometimes we are so desperate, we'll put up with a lot of unnecessary stuff just to have a man around," Adria confessed delicately. "But the truth is, some men are just not very nice to women ... no matter what."

Adria gazed out the passenger car window and prepared herself for the next thought.

"Bryson, may I ask you a question." Adria continued to look out the windshield.

"Sure." She could hear the caution in his voice.

"Are you aware of the fact you are considered a womanizer?"

"A womanizer? Yep. Most people also call me a whore or a fornicator," Bryson laughed.

Adria was taken aback by his flippant attitude. To her, this was not a funny topic at all.

"Really, why?" asked Adria.

"Because when I first came on board at GFCC, I went out a lot to get to know people and ran into a few problems with the women in the church. I guess I was fresh meat," Bryson laughed nervously. "However, I have not slept with every woman in this church. I have gone out with a few of them, some more than once and have had sex with only two within the past three years of service. Bishop and I had a discussion about it, and he was extremely vocal about his expectations. Then I decided to lay low, because the interactions were making me look bad," Bryson admitted. "I straightened up my act and I have grown a lot. I am not a saint, but I have changed in many ways."

"How did it make you look bad?" Adria inquired further.

"The women talked about our dates, what we did and compared notes, and it became increasingly harder for me," Bryson admitted. "Bishop does not like scandals of any kind, especially on his ministerial board."

Adria's Transformation

Adria thought about his response, and the honesty behind it. She wasn't a saint either and couldn't judge him for his past actions. But she also appreciated that he had matured.

"Was it what was bothering you earlier ... before the movie?" Bryson inquired.

"Yes, it was some of it. The other part was my sister," Adria confessed with a sigh. "She's always had a way of getting to me. I think she has a problem with me just being happy. I think she wants to keep punishing me."

"Punishing you for what?"

"For ... being a heathen for a while and not being around much to pay attention to her," Adria replied. "When I moved away, it really negatively impacted her."

Bryson made a dramatic face.

"Just what kind of heathen were you? And why do you let her punish you?" he asked.

"It's a long and very complicated story," Adria responded, but didn't offer to share it. Not yet. "One day, we will talk more about it."

Even still, she wondered how long it would take for Bryson to probe deeply into her years away from Rockville. What would she do if he wanted more details of the decade away from home? How much would Adria be willing to share?

"I guess we both have a past," was all he said though.

"I certainly don't want to compare notes. I am just glad God gives us second and third chances," Adria added and smiled.

"I heard that," Bryson stated as he pulled into the property of the restaurant and found a parking space. "Now, let's go in and enjoy a nice dinner."

"So, when are you two getting married?" Jerome asked Bryson and Adria.

"We are just getting started," Adria quickly chimed in with her eyes widened.

"You already look like a married couple; you might as well admit it, you are pretty well connected," Jerome offered and remained focused on his dinner while he made the statement.

"You think so?" Adria questioned.

Jerome looked into Adria's eyes before he responded, "Oh yeah, you two are very comfortable with each other. You are comfortable in each other's space. Have you had your first argument yet?"

"No," Bryson answered.

"Then don't get married before you had at least one good argument, so it will *not* be a surprise," Jerome advised. "People in our church get married really quick, and they didn't have their first real argument before they got married and they have a time trying to figure things out after they say, 'I do'."

"He is right," Millicent affirmed. "The first argument tells you a whole lot about each other. As a matter of fact, I suggest you have two of them as it uncovers some topics you need to know how to handle. Though, you might not get over the second one so quickly," Millicent admitted with an attitude and a pointer finger raised for emphasis. "Then after those two arguments you will really know how much you love each other. When all those emotions get tested, you will know," Millicent added in a stern tone.

"Also," Jerome stated, "And this one is a hard one, but if you are selfish or self-centered, marriage was going to be a great learning lesson for you, especially when you have kids."

Jerome and Millicent continued to share dating and marriage advice, learned through their mentorship roles at GFCC and their own personal scenarios. Adria looked up at Val and Alton at times who nodded affirmatively at insight and support. She listened intently, but noted how several times throughout the dinner, Bryson's phone would illuminate, indicating an incoming call or text. He glanced at the screen a couple of times and then ignored them. Eventually he flipped the phone over so it would no longer be a distraction.

While Adria was accustomed to Bryson receiving phone calls from his family and his musical team members, tonight, she was extra sensitive to the interruptions. Starting to feel anxious again, Adria wanted to ask Bryson about it, but she managed her emotions. It didn't stop her curiosity and only served to make her even more suspicious about the 'intruder' and skeptical about Bryson.

Dr. Paula Y. Obie

Chapter 6
The One Night Stand

At the end of the dinner, during the ride home, Bryson announced he had a task list that needed his undivided attention so he would get going. He walked her to the door, kissed her lovingly on the lips and said, "I will give you a call before bedtime, if it is not too late."

She agreed. He bade her good night and walked back to his car. He backed out of the driveway and drove a few minutes from Adria's home, before he turned into a fast-food restaurant parking lot. Now, he could give his phone his undivided attention. During the dinner, when the calls and texts were received, Bryson simply ignored them, but he also understood that his conversation with Adria about his reputation had made receiving these phone calls more awkward for him. He had nothing to hide, but he also now had something to lose.

Bryson had received several calls and texts from the same phone number, but it was not a number he recognized, as his family, musical team and Bishop were all saved in his address book. One text message simply stated, 'Call ASAP!'

He responded to one of the texts with simply, "Who is this?"

"Mary...," came the return text.

He had removed her from his contact list months ago.

"Please, it's urgent," she followed up with.

Bryson sighed and dialed her number.

"Can you come over?" Mary asked. "Like I said in the messages, this is very important."

Even though the feeling in his gut signaled there was trouble ahead, Bryson felt this would be better handled in person, rather than over the phone. She could say whatever she had to say, and he could tell her that he was no longer available for her to text or call.

"Sure," Bryson responded. "I am just a few minutes away."

Bryson arrived at Mary's house, rang the doorbell and she ushered him into her residence.

"Come in," Mary stated. "Can I get you anything?" Her voice was cool, indifferent.

"No, I am fine," Bryson responded and took a seat in the chair near the door. He felt the tension in the room. He had not visited in several months, and even then, he hadn't spent much time with her. Bryson tried to remain calm, but he couldn't get the notion out of his head that he was walking into something bad. He had to protect himself somehow and before he rang the doorbell, he placed his phone on silent mode and pressed the 'record' button on the voice recorder. Now, with the phone tucked away in his pocket, he waited.

Mary sat down on the couch beside the chair near Bryson. She looked at him briefly before speaking, "I am five months pregnant, and the baby is yours."

Bryson glared into Mary's eyes; unsure he had heard her correctly.

"You're pregnant...?"

Adria's Transformation

"Five months, and the baby is yours," she repeated.

Bryson thought back to that night. This wasn't possible. "We only had sex one time and I was wearing protection," he stated calmly. "You told me you were on birth control, remember?"

"It only takes one time and I guess our birth control methods did not work," Mary replied.

Bryson was speechless. He tried to find reason for all this but couldn't make sense of it. She was pregnant...with his child? What about Adria?

"Why did you not tell me about this sooner?" Bryson enquired emotionless.

"I just found out. I don't have regular periods, so I was not entirely sure I was pregnant," Mary said. "I went to the doctor because I had not been feeling well. He performed a pregnancy test and confirmed I am five months pregnant."

Mary then handed Bryson a copy of the notes from her doctor's visit stating she was indeed pregnant. He looked intently at the paperwork.

Still unable to wrap his mind around what was happening, all Bryson could say was, "And you are saying the child was mine?"

"Yes, you and I had sex five months ago and you are the only man I had slept with in over two years," Mary responded. Bryson could hear the weariness in her tone, as if she had simply expected him to accept what she was saying. "It is your child, Bryson."

Even after hearing the repeated words several times, Bryson still couldn't register them. They didn't seem real. He needed proof.

"Can you take a DNA test?" Bryson requested. "I will pay for it."

Mary's anger was inflamed by this.

"What are you saying, Bryson?"

Feeling like he was finally coming to his senses, he said, "I need proof the child is mine. I will take care of this child...," Bryson continued, and then amended his statement, "*If* this child is mine, I will take care of him or her, just like I take care of Duane. I just need to know it's mine."

Mary stood up and glared angrily at Bryson before speaking, "*If?! If?!* Are you calling me a liar?"

The situation was escalating faster than Bryson could keep up with and he tried to calm her. He stood up and said, "Listen, Mary, it's been months..."

"No. I called you over here to give you an opportunity to step up as a man and do the right thing, but this is what you do? You accuse me of lying to you? I'm so sick and tired of all you Black brothers, making babies, but not taking responsibility—"

He grew angry at her persistence and cut her off.

"What do you expect me to do? We were never a couple," he exclaimed, his voice raised. "You call me after five months and expect me to drop everything and just accept his? And then what? Marry you?"

Mary's face contorted in shock.

"So now you are willing to shame me into being a single mother?" Mary cried, "How dare you be so cold! I will call everyone, make sure they know what kind of man you really are."

Those words hit Bryson hardest. What would happen when Bishop heard about this? He had given him zero chances to have any more situations with women that would embarrass himself, and the church. Or his family? Mom and Pop Kenton—what would their reactions be?

Adria's Transformation

What about Adria? His heart hurt at the thought of her finding out. He cringed at the thought of how this would impact her, how it would hurt her.

"Mary—"

But she wasn't listening anymore.

"I don't have to deal with this in my own house. Get out!" Mary angrily pointed to the door. "If you don't get out, right now, I am going to call the police."

Bryson looked at her sternly and then he walked out of the door and into his car. He reached into his jacket, retrieved his phone, and stopped the recording.

Bryson was in shock. He was suspicious when he received the repeated calls and texts requesting a return call ASAP. But he was not prepared for this type of news.

"Why now? Why tonight?" Bryson asked himself during the ride home.

He thought about his time with Mary. They had not dated and were never in a relationship. What they had was just supposed to be fun. He had been over to see her a couple of times. On the last evening, they got closer and had sex. It was around Valentine's Day, and it was the only time they were intimate. He knew afterwards it was a mistake and didn't follow up with her. But Mary continued to invite him over. He kept declining her invitations, not at all interested pursuing a relationship with her.

For a while, she was obsessive, calling several times a day and sending multiple text messages. However, he never responded to her, and she soon stopped communicating. He had not had any interaction with Mary since then...until today.

Bryson felt his stomach lurch. His life would be in turmoil if it turned out he was the father of this child.

Even though he had worked diligently to be a more responsible man, his past was seemingly catching up with him.

Bryson's eyes darted back and forth, as he tried to focus on driving. All his senses were heightened. Slowly he felt his anger consume every cell of his body and his face. His anger at himself fueled him even more as he motored into his driveway and his garage.

Now home, he slowly walked inside and dropped onto the couch. He blew air loudly and rubbed his face with both of his hands. He could feel his heart beating fast in his chest. He was at a total loss for words and his head now felt as if someone had a jackhammer and was pounding on his temples. Bryson placed his fingers to both sides of his head and began to gently rub them. His thoughts returned to Adria and Duane, who were the closest to him right now. He then looked at his hands—hands God had blessed him with to pen music and play instruments. He felt ashamed of how he had been using them.

Bryson reached for his phone to call Tara. Whenever he was in trouble, it was his sister in whom he confided. He needed her now.

"Hello brother!" Tara answered cheerfully, "How are you? Are you on your way?"

Bryson gently tapped the middle of his forehead with his fist.

"Oh, I am sorry, I am running a little late, I will be there soon," Bryson mumbled. He had forgotten that Tara was babysitting Duane. He picked up his keys and phone and walked out into the garage. At least this way, he could speak face to face with her.

Adria's Transformation

Once Bryson arrived at his sister Tara's house, he immediately shared with her the news from Mary. Bryson shared the details of the phone calls and showed her the texts he received at the restaurant. He also shared the details of the face-to-face visit with Mary. Tara's face became increasingly saddened, and she slowly sat down on her sofa.

"Oh, wow," Tara responded slowly. She paused, then added, "I am at a loss for words."

Tara and Bryson remained quiet for a few minutes and then she sat up with an intentional look on her face and declared, "Well, we will get through this. I didn't even know you dated Mary. You never talked about her."

"I wasn't dating her," Bryson responded.

He stared at his sister and offered a saddened, yet cold look. It was so different from his cheerful disposition from earlier when he dropped off Duane. It was just a few hours ago when he was happy and full of smiles. Now that had all changed.

"Listen, brother, you need to talk to Adria now," Tara suggested. "I will take care of Duane for tonight."

"I am not ready to talk to Adria yet," Bryson replied. "I need to think about this some more. Duane can come home with me."

"Okay, but don't wait too long. This kind of news travels fast," Tara warned.

Bryson nodded and proceeded to collect a sleepy Duane. He drove back to his residence. He carried Duane slowly into the house and prepared him for bed. Bryson then sat on the edge of the bed and watched as his son fell back asleep with his favorite toy gripped tightly in his right hand.

Bryson returned to his bedroom, his mind racing with thoughts about the plans that had to be made if he was to be a father again. He had been in a committed relationship with Rheta when she got pregnant. He wanted to marry her. This new situation was totally different—this was a one-night stand, and he had no intentions at all of proposing marriage to Mary just because she was pregnant.

He sighed. He needed to make at least one phone call tonight—to Bishop to schedule an appointment for them to meet.

Bryson needed to talk to Alton as well to prepare him for possible changes in his musical responsibilities at church. After that, he would talk to Adria, face-to-face. He desired to send her a text message now to say good night but changed his mind.

After coordinating a meeting with Bishop, Bryson showered and prepared himself for bed. But he was too restless to sleep.

Bryson's dream was always to get married first, with a big wedding and eventually have as many children as he and his wife could afford—at least three children but possibly five if she agreed to the proposition. It was never his desire to start his family before the marriage, but that was the way things worked out.

Now, four years later, he had found himself in a more complex situation. He was in love again with a woman who he envisioned as one who would be a true helpmate and an amazing mother to their children. But the news he received tonight was going to have a negative impact on their new relationship. Hoping to salvage that, Bryson finally typed a text message to Adria.

"Goodnight luv!" he simply wrote.

Adria's Transformation

It took Adria only a few minutes to send a similar text response.

Then he prayed himself to sleep.

Dr. Paula Y. Obie

Chapter 7
Lord, Help Me!

"Minister Bryson," Bishop stated the next day. Bryson's meeting with him was scheduled after the morning services and the Pastor's luncheon. "We had an agreement you would not cause any of these types of scandals which involved women. This also included the situation where you would not become a father again outside of marriage. Do you remember our agreement?"

"Yes, Bishop, I remember the agreement," Bryson answered quietly as he nodded his head affirmatively.

"Then are you prepared to marry this girl if she is pregnant with your child? Or are you prepared to resign your position as Minister of Music if you are not willing to marry the mother of your child?"

"Yes, Bishop, I am prepared to honor my agreement with the church," Bryson responded. "I have asked for a paternity test and stated I would pay for it, but the request was not well received."

"I see," Bishop responded. "Unfortunately, the young lady was not the one who made the agreement with GFCC, it was you. So, son, I pray this all works out for you."

Bryson nodded in agreement as the meeting continued. In the end, Bishop prayed for his Minister of Music and gave him a hug.

Bishop had reminded him he had not committed a crime and would not go to jail for fathering two children by two different women. Still, he couldn't shake the feeling that he had done something wrong. After all, GFCC had standards and he was a church leader. He had to have integrity and display the character of the church detailed in the leadership guidelines. If Bryson were indeed the father, he would be taken to the GFCC Board for the next steps in the process.

In some church denominations, a minister in this type of situation (a child out of wedlock) would be sat down for a certain period. They would be able to return to their post after a time of reflection and repentance. However, this situation differed in that it could be his second child outside of marriage. Bryson totally understood his accountability and accepted the consequences of his actions. But he should have known better.

Bryson's greatest concern at this very moment, was Adria and the possibility of losing the first woman he has loved in years. He decided to speak to Adria next.

Bryson sighed heavily and picked up the phone to call Adria's number as he was driving.

"Hi darling!" Bryson said when she answered.

"Church was good," Adria said. "I didn't see you and Duane there."

Bryson didn't respond to her question, but asked, "Can I come over? Maybe we can get take-out, if you have not eaten."

"Of course," Adria stated. She hesitated and asked, "Is everything okay?"

"See you soon!" Bryson replied quickly, as if he hadn't heard her and ended the call.

ୡ

Adria stared down at her phone. Yesterday had been one of those strange days that left her feeling out of sorts. But when Bryson and Duane did not attend service, she grew even more concerned. Adria couldn't help but feel a little anxious as she waited for Bryson to arrive. But even that didn't alleviate her concerns. When Bryson walked into the house, he had a firm look on his face. He gave Adria a quick kiss and paced throughout the living room.

Adria sat on the ottoman and watched him walk back and forth for a few minutes before he finally perched himself on the floor and positioned his body at an angle where he looked Adria squarely in the eye and grabbed her hands. She braced herself. This was a serious matter.

"Adria, you know that I love you dearly, right?" Bryson started. "Before I go on, I want you to know that is how I feel. I am deeply in love with you, and I want you to know it."

"Okay, I know," Adria replied cautiously.

"Last night, in the restaurant, I received a number of urgent phone calls and text messages. When I returned the call, I was told I was going to be a father again..."

Adria stared intently at Bryson as he told his story. It took all her inner strength to maintain her composure. Inwardly though, her mind raced as she experienced each emotion. She felt anger, frustration, shock, and grief in a matter of seconds, with the cycle repeating itself over and over as Bryson spoke about the consequences of his dilemma, including the impact it could have on his job at the church. He was visibly sorrowful and although she felt badly for him, her heart was breaking, and she wasn't sure what she should do.

"Talk to me about the relationship," Adria eventually said, when Bryson came to the end of his story. She was devoid of emotion, afraid to feel. "Were you dating?"

"No. We became friends during one of the multimedia church campaigns. I went over to her place a couple of times," Bryson reflected. "And one night, we got too comfortable and ended up being intimate."

"So, it was casual sex with a friend?" Adria asked stoically.

"Pretty much," Bryson answered and paused, awaiting the next question.

"Did you wear protection?" Adria had a list of questions that she was going to ask no matter what.

"Yes, I did, but I guess it didn't matter," he replied gently.

"Were you the only guy she was sleeping with?"

"She says I was the only one."

"Do you believe her?"

"I don't have a reason to doubt her, but the truth is, I don't know," Bryson said.

"Why is she just telling you this now?" Adria asked sternly. She could feel her anger rising, she just wasn't sure who she was angry with. "I mean, she's been pregnant for several months, right?"

Adria looked away and tried to pull her hands from Bryson's grip. She felt the sudden need to flee, but he held on even tighter.

"Adria, please listen to me," Bryson begged her. "I am really, really sorry. I just don't know how to make this right with you."

Adria's Transformation

Adria tried hard to maintain her calm, but she couldn't do it anymore. She pulled her hands out of his and exclaimed, "What do you want me to say?! Bryson, I don't have any rights here! I am not important in this scenario. What do you want me to say?"

"You are important to me ... very important to me." Bryson declared.

"But this is not about me. It doesn't matter what I feel or don't feel. You, the mother, your unborn child—that's what matters, not me and ..."

Adria's lip quivered as her voice trailed off. She tried hard not to cry, but the tears flowed without her permission. She was losing Bryson after having just found him.

Bryson pulled Adria into a hug and said, "Please don't cry, baby." He held her tightly, and she let him while she tried to process her emotions. After a few minutes of crying, the tears started to abate, and they both settled down on the floor in front of the couch.

"Are you going to take a paternity test?" Adria asked through her tears.

"Yes, I am," Bryson replied.

Adria hesitated before asking her next question.

"If the child is yours, will you marry her?"

Bryson pondered the question but didn't look at her.

"If I marry her, I can keep my job at the church and do the right thing as a man and as a dad. If I do not marry her, then I must resign my job at GFCC and do the right thing and be a dad—again—and not please God or my faith," Bryson said quietly, as if weighing his options.

Adria looked up at the ceiling and sighed deeply, as if to say, "Oh God!"

"If I marry her," Bryson continued, "Then I'll be marrying someone I don't love, and I will be in love with someone else..."

"But then you would do what is right in the eyes of God," Adria whispered.

"I would also be living a lie," Bryson responded, soberly. He finally looked at her and said, "It's too complicated for me to make any types of decisions tonight. Can I count on you to remain in my corner and be my friend?"

"Friend?" Adria gasped, "I think it is way too soon for me to be making any commitments. I don't even know what to feel right now, Bryson, I really don't."

He opened his mouth to say something, but she cut him off.

"I am not naïve," Adria said sharply. "I know this happens all the time, but now it has happened to me. Bryson, I am no saint, and I will be the last person to sit here in judgment. I just feel like someone kicked me in the gut and it hurts, and I don't think it's fair for you to ask this of me."

"I don't think that I can stand to lose you and my Minister of Music's job on the same day ... so, maybe we can table this for now?" Bryson suggested.

Adria glared at him, unsure what to say. For the last few weeks, she felt like she was on top of the world. Now She felt like the world was on top of her.

But nothing was certain yet. She couldn't make a final decision not knowing all the details. Plus, wasn't she the one always talking about second and third chances?

Seeing her indecision, Bryson again said, "Babe, I am really, really sorry about this. I want you to know I would never do anything to intentionally hurt you."

Adria's Transformation

"I believe you," was all she verbalized softly. And she did.

The next day, Adria woke up with a massive headache. She had not slept well the night before. She tossed and turned after Bryson left and felt like she had just drifted off to sleep when the alarm sounded.

Adria groaned as she forced herself to get out of bed and prepare for work. Under normal circumstances, her work environment was always a great place for her to focus, but today was different. It was a struggle to prepare for work and pretend she was okay, even though her personal life was now in turmoil.

Adria and her business partner, Carla Hinton, were supposed to be meeting with their admin Yvonne, but Adria had called Carla prior to coming into work and gave her highlights of the dilemma. They agreed to cancel the meeting and talk in the office.

"I know it is way too early, but what are you going to do if all of this does not work out in your favor?" Carla asked.

"I have no idea," Adria responded, shaking her head. She turned away from Carla and stared out the window. "I am so angry; I could just scream."

Carla got up from the chair and walked to the sofa to retrieve one of the pillows. She returned to her chair and handed it to Adria.

"Go for it!" Carla demanded. "The pillow will catch the sound, or you could always do a silent scream."

Adria grabbed the pillow and placed it over her face and screamed as loud as she could into it. She was beyond tears; she was furious, disappointed, and frustrated. It felt good to release the scream, but she didn't feel any better about her situation.

"You are just going to have to take it a day at a time," Carla stated. "But don't forget to look out for yourself. And you know I am here for you." Carla reached over and rubbed her friend's back. She checked her smart watch and added, "I have a call in ten minutes. I'm going to jump on that, but I will check in with you afterwards. Let me know if you want me to do the video call then maybe you can take the rest of the day off...?"

Adria shrugged her shoulders before she murmured, "Okay." After Carla left, Adria walked over to the desk and phoned Yvonne asking her to cancel and reschedule all of her appointments for the day as she was getting ready to leave.

Adria wasn't ready to go home yet, though. Adria understood it was her place of serenity and peace, and the place she needed to be. There, she could change into comfortable clothes and start pulling herself and her splintered emotions back to a more healed place. But right now, it was the last place she wanted to be.

Way deep down inside, Adria wished she could pick up the phone and talk to her mother, but Mama Darden would not be sympathetic. She would get furious, quote fifty scriptures, act like she had never sinned and forget her role was to comfort her daughter. Adria was not in the mood for this type of letdown...again. Their relationship was certainly better than when Adria first left, but it would never be what Adria imagined what it should be.

Then Adria thought of Douglas. She reached for her phone and texted him asking if he was free for an early

Adria's Transformation

lunch. And like the guardian angel he was, he made himself available.

The two friends agreed to meet at Café Pastaria!

The waitress directed them to their table and took their beverage orders.

"Thanks for texting me for lunch," Douglas stated, "I was trying to figure out where I was going to eat. Although, as you know my lunch hour is normally at 1:00 p.m. I will definitely need a To Go box for when I get hungry later." Douglas raised his eyes from the menu to glance at Adria, but she did not chuckle at his food joke.

The waiter came to take their lunch orders and then disappeared out of hearing range.

"So, what's up?" Douglas finally asked.

Adria sighed deeply.

"I don't really know where to begin...," she stated sipping on her water. She didn't want to make this real by talking about it, but she really needed to talk. "Do you remember when you mentioned that there were rumors about Bryson and his dating habits?" Adria asked as she looked into Douglas' eyes.

"Yes...," Douglas replied with hesitation.

"Well, we may be in trouble, as one of those dates...before us, of course...turned into a possible... well, ... whatever ...the girl is pregnant, and she says it's his child." Adria had started the sentence with a professional tone, but she quickly changed her tone and blurted out the words.

"Wow!" Douglas replied calmly.

"Who is the girl?" Douglas asked, then changed his mind. "Wait ... forget the question, how are you?"

"Mad as twenty-five firecrackers, but I am not going to lose it until I find out the facts," Adria declared.

"The facts?" Douglas asked.

"Yes, Bryson said he only slept with her once. They weren't dating, and they just got cozy *one* time...," Adria added.

"Well, for some, it takes only one time," Douglas said, matter-of-factly. And he was right, but this wasn't what she wanted to hear right now. Douglas seemed to sense that and asked, "When did you find out all of this?"

"Yesterday."

"Oh," Douglas responded. "How far along is she? Did she just find out?"

"That's the thing, supposedly it happened five months ago. She's five months pregnant but she's just telling him about it now," Adria spouted out. "Now, we wait for the DNA test... if she takes one. And then I really have a lot to think about...and just as we were starting on this relationship journey...," Adria ended the sentence with an audible sigh.

"I am so sorry. This was not cool at all," Douglas said after a minute, as if to ensure there was nothing else she wanted to add. "Not cool at all, but..."

"But what?" Adria inquired.

"You don't know for sure it is his, so you have to just wait patiently," Douglas added. "You are a very patient person, Adria."

Adria shook her head.

"I don't know if that is true anymore." She looked around the restaurant. "I am just not sure if I have what it takes to be with him, if this child was his, Douglas. I am not that kind of girl."

"What kind of girl?"

Adria tapped her well-manicured fingers on the table before returning attention to her food and her friend.

Adria's Transformation

"The kind to just put up with all types of scenarios, just because," Adria explained.

"That's understandable."

She took a deep breath and turned back to her friend.

"What else do you know?" he asked.

"I really don't know anything else. She called him, told him the news and now we are trying to deal with it," Adria stated.

"Is this someone you know?" Douglas inquired.

"I know *of* her," Adria replied and then looked at Douglas, "She and Francine are friends."

"Oh, I see."

"I just don't understand why she would wait until she was five months pregnant before telling Bryson," Adria blurted out, "I mean, what kind of relationship did they really have?"

"Are you doubting what Bryson told you?" Douglas asked.

"No. I don't know. Right now, I am just angry and disappointed," Adria added. "Do you realize if the child is Bryson's, he will have two children by two different women and then there would be me? And if we got married and had our own child or children, they would be a third, plus, and then it would be me? This was not something I planned at all. I am being selfish and do not want to share him with anyone else."

"Well," Douglas added, "At least you are willing to face it head on and are not looking the other way."

"Yes, I learned my lesson about being truly honest about the people and the situations to whom I connect," Adria said bitterly.

"When was that?"

"When I was with J. But me and him...I was not J's only girlfriend, and I knew that. He had a number of them, and they loved to brag about it. But he always told me I was his number one." Adria stressed this point by lifting her pointer finger. "You would have never known when we were in the club that he and I were together. We were very discrete, on purpose."

"You never told me that .... humph!" Douglas added as he quickly dropped both sides of his mouth.

"I really appreciated him because he gave me the opportunity to just live my own life. My relationship with him was easy, because I knew I was not the only girl—and it was okay by me. I enjoyed his company, and I loved the freedom! I *never* had any kind of freedom to just do what I wanted." Adria added. "Just being able to go to a club and have a good time was new to me because enjoying life was not a part of my world. I think it was why our relationship grew the way it did."

Adria paused as she considered her journey.

"But that wasn't healthy. There was stuff I did... I put my head in the sand and looked the other way because of my relationship with J...Then, I come home and meet Bryson," Adria said, started to get upset again, "And really fall in love and now this!"

Douglas reached out and took her hand.

"It's too early to come to any conclusions with the baby situation. Don't do that." He looked at his phone to check the time. "Do you want me to call into work and request off? We can hang out for the rest of the day,"

Douglas' offer was sincere, and Adria was tempted to accept it, but knew she really wanted to just be alone for a while.

Adria's Transformation

"No," Adria sighed, "I need to just go home, relax my mind, and do nothing today. You can call me later if you want."

"You got it!" Douglas confirmed. "Just promise me you will look out for yourself. Remember Bryson is not J, and you can still do whatever you want. I think you have buried the old Adria but buried is where she needs to stay. Give this is the new Adria's turn at life!"

After the lunch with Douglas, Adria felt even more fatigued and went home to decompress, and find some peace.

Bryson called to check in and they spoke briefly; however, neither one of them really had a lot to say other than just reaching out and connecting. The phone call only lasted a few minutes and while she was happy to hear his voice, wanting things to go back the way they were, she couldn't help replaying everything she had learned in the last day. Adria flooded her mind with positive self-talk to keep the thoughts at bay, but it was taking a lot of focus, mental strength, and lots and lots of prayer. She thought that would be enough to help her through this. Then the thought hit her: *Mary is Francine's friend!* Hadn't Francine said as much during their last call? Adria was certain Francine was already aware of the intricate details of this situation. And she, no doubt, had already shared the news with their entire family. How in the world was Adria going to deal with this one...?

Dr. Paula Y. Obie

Chapter 8
Broken But Healing

Later that week, against her better judgement, Adria took a call from Francine. She wanted to know what her sister would say about Bryson and Mary, but Francine only talked about herself and current family events. Adria thought she might have been mistaken about her sister's association with Mary, but when she started bringing up the past, Adria decided it wasn't worth finding out. Already frayed by the events of the past few days, she decided simply to end the call.

"I have to go now Francine, I will call you later," she said and hung up, though she had no intention of keeping her word.

Francine and Adria were polar opposites. Francine loudly verbalized her feelings, while Adria was more introspective and buried her emotions deep inside. And when she reached her peak and had enough of a situation then she became extremely angry. This was the moment when the scenario heightened and became chaotic. That's what happened the day she left.

Francine often referred to Adria's moving away from the family as abandonment, her being melodramatic and self-centered, but Adria preferred to think of it as gaining her freedom, it was her way of surviving. At that very moment, on that day, Adria felt that if she just stayed one more hour—no one more minute, in the situation she was in, she would not be able to breathe. She had to move away from home so she could be her own person, and not live a life controlled by others, controlled by Mama Darden.

Of course, that's not how they saw it.

"Remember, you left us ... you made your choice, remember? You could have just stayed and fought for your rights, but you chose to run instead," Francine often reminded her, but she knew she wouldn't have made it if she had stayed.

At that moment, Adria's phone rang—her customized ring tone identified the caller as her mother.

"She must feel I am thinking about her," Adria said to herself. While Francine had said nothing about Bryson, Adria couldn't help but wonder at the coincidental timing of the call. Unlike her decision to talk to Francine, Adria opted to ignore her mother and allow the message to go into her voice mail, knowing Mama Darden was not a fan of leaving messages and would simply hang up.

Growing up, Adria was non-confrontational and never understood how to effectively stand up for herself. If she wanted to respond to a tense situation, then she would overdo it and engage in lecture-style or lawyer-style responses not welcomed in their household. She would get lost in the faces of her Mother and Francine and stop talking as she always felt it was a waste of her time. After a while, when it seemed her wants and needs fell on deaf ears, Adria retreated from communicating to

Adria's Transformation

reading books. She stopped trying to communicate with her mother and sister.

It seemed even in her return, somethings didn't change.

"Ugh!" Adria yelled, gazing up at the ceiling, "This was what I came back for?" Adria screamed aloud and then mumbled, "Things were going okay for me ... well sorta ... I was somewhat content... kind of...and now this. What exactly what do I have to do to just have a happy life?"

Adria thought about herself as a fourteen-year-old, young, energetic teenager who, two years later, had become more calloused and withdrawn from life. She had stopped communicating and found herself going through the motions—services on Sunday, choir rehearsal on Monday, youth Bible study on Wednesday and meetings on Saturday. There were a few school gatherings she was allowed to attend if they did not interfere with her church appointments. Her social life mostly revolved around church and in-school activities only. No other social activities were allowed. She had very little fun, no genuine friendships, and no voice to speak of.

Adria's sheltered life protected her from drug and, alcohol abuse, from promiscuity and teenage pregnancy. But she had minimal social skills and became a gullible person. Adria only really had one skill and that was managing church-related activities, all under the watchful eye of Mama Darden.

It was at Adria's college graduation party when she felt something begin to boil to surface. The night was festive, the food was amazing, and she had a lot of envelopes in her hands.

Once the celebration ended, the gifts were gathered, and the family left the restaurant. The Darden's met at the homeplace, and everything seemed normal. It should have been a very jubilant time, a rite of passage, a monumental achievement as she was the first in her family to graduate from a four-year college, but everything changed the next day.

Mama Darden prepared a scrumptious luncheon. Papa Darden, Francine, Adria and two of the brothers were in attendance. In the middle of the meal, Mama Darden announced to Adria she would be handling all of her college graduate monetary gifts as she knew she would "just throw it all away." She also told Adria she made arrangements for her to take a position at the Executive Leader's office as an administrative assistant, during the time she was searching for a suitable job.

"You will not get paid," Mama Darden announced, "However, it is an opportunity for you to give back to the church which was so supportive of you while you were in school."

Mama Darden took out a paper and pen and began to review the list of changes scheduled to take place, now that Adria was a college graduate.

Adria looked down at the plate of food in front of her, and desperately wanted to argue her way out of taking the volunteer job assignment. However, the Executive Top Leaders were responsible for her earning multiple yearly scholarships while she attended college. They also arranged to send Adria monetary gifts throughout her college life to ensure she never had need of anything. She couldn't refuse them, but she couldn't keep living her life the way other people wanted her to live it.

Adria's Transformation

Adria felt the tension growing in the atmosphere but rather than argue, she ignored her mother's comments and said, "Mama, I want to get one of my checks as I really need to take a vacation before I start working."

"A vacation for what?" Mama Darden asked, "You think you gonna go down to that beach and make a fool out of yourself? Well, no ma'am, you are going to work!"

Adria had no immediate reaction. Surely, she had heard her mother wrong and had misunderstood her. She continued to speak.

"A few of the graduates made plans for a trip and it sounds like a lot of fun before everyone started working," Adria persisted, as she took a sip from her beverage glass and continued eating her lunch.

"The answer is 'No'," Mama Darden declared.

"But there should be more than enough money for me to have a little fun, as I have not done anything in four years," Adria continued. "I don't need much, maybe one thousand dollars or fifteen hundred."

"A thousand dollars?" Mama Darden inquired with a gaze of astonishment, glancing at Adria's face momentarily before continuing to eat. "Well, I can tell you after the graduation dinner last night, and the costs of all of your graduation requirements, you do not have more than a few hundred dollars left," Mama Darden spoke calmly.

Adria frowned. There was more in there than that. The college graduation expenses, the invitations, the college ring, etc. and graduation celebration were indeed costly. However, there were several thousands in the account two months earlier. She looked at Mama Darden and while she wanted to know what happened to all the money in there, she decided this conversation would have to wait until another time.

The storm in her chest was growing stronger, but somehow, she maintained her composure.

Mama Darden then placed down her fork and looked at Adria. "And can you tell me why you stopped going out with Shawn D? He is such a nice boy, and his parents are just great people. They absolutely love you!"

Adria flushed at the mention of his name.

"We went out a couple of times," Adria said with trepidation.

"What, so he's not good enough for you, now you are a college graduate, and he couldn't finish his schooling?" Mama Darden asked. "College was supposed to make you smart, but not make you a snob, Adria."

"Maybe she just doesn't like the boy, Mama," Papa Darden interjected. "Just leave it alone."

The pressure in her chest was rising to yet another level of intensity and Adria tried hard to maintain her composure, but Mama Darden was making it difficult. She was picking a fight. The Adria sitting at the table was not in the mood to fight. On the outside, she appeared calm and composed, but everything inside of her was in turmoil.

"I have invited him over for dinner tonight, so you two could get better acquainted," Mama Darden announced.

"I have plans tonight and won't be here," Adria replied without looking away from her plate. She placed a small portion of the food on her fork and prepared to take another bite.

"Well, you are just going to have to cancel or reschedule them, as you two young people need to learn

Adria's Transformation

how to sit down and have a proper conversation. I have already talked to the Lord about this, and I really need to help you out because you act like you don't know what you are doing."

Adria looked up from her plate and then darted her eyes first at her father and then at Francine. Her brothers had left to go to a sporting event, leaving them there to deal with the situation. Adria felt the temperature in the room getting hotter. She wanted to be respectful, but at the same time, she could not kowtow to her mother.

"No, Mama, I can't change my plans for tonight. And I am not interested in Shawn D at all," Adria said, firmly, "And neither is he interested in me," she added quietly.

It was the tone of Adria's voice to get the attention of those sitting at the table.

"Oh, so, I guess you are all grown now, Ms. College Graduate, and can make all of your decisions," her mother reacted sarcastically.

Adria looked up at Mama Darden. She wanted to remain impassive, but everything was boiling up to the surface. Still, she maintained control and tried to reason with her mother.

"I am in an adult body, and I have an adult age, yes, but I am so naïve, I don't even know what to do at times. I get so lost and although the world thinks I can function as an adult, I am like a child, because I have never been allowed to make a decision on my own. I asked you about the money and what was it you said? No? I worked hard for those gifts. I should be able to enjoy it this one time. These four years have been a lot of hard work..."

Mama Darden flipped her hands in the air as if to disregard Adria's pleas. It was her usual sign she had heard enough.

Adria had had enough as well. Unaware of her action, she rose from her chair and was standing and using the edge of the dining table as support, holding onto the table's edge with both hands.

"Mother, I am sorry, but I am so tired of listening about what you want!" Adria blurted out.

"Do not talk to me that way, young lady!" Mama Darden responded angrily.

"Mom, you talk about Shawn D, and you don't even know him. Again, I am the one who was too dumb to even realize how easily a person can be taken advantage of! He was just using me .... that's all it was."

Francine and Papa Darden stared at Adria and Mama Darden for a few minutes. It was if they had momentarily frozen into their positions. Papa Darden placed his fork down on the table and dropped his hands into his lap. Francine glared at her sister chewing her food slowly.

"Adria, just sit down and eat your food," Papa Darden pleaded.

Adria looked at her father and then at her mother. "Poppie, you don't get it...Mama, you don't get it... I was too naïve and dumb to know how much he was going to use me... Yes, use me! You can talk about how dependable and good he is, how he can do no wrong, but he's not who you think he is. Here's the truth of the matter...," Adria started to shake nervously from the tension of the conversation. She had not mentioned any of this to anyone at home because of who his parents were, but now she needed to say something. "He violated me!"

Adria saw her parents visibly freeze up at that revelation. But she was too worked up to stop now.

"Yes, the son of your dear friends raped me. I guess the word 'no' does not mean 'no' to some people. I was humiliated by your Shawn D. You wanna know what he said to me? He said, 'You church girls are all alike, you are just too dumb to know what life is all about. You are easy and desperate.' Shawn D is nothing but a big liar and manipulator and I do not want to see him ever again!"

The tension in the room was heavier than it was before. Papa Darden had a look of shock on his face and Francine was speechless with no expression. But it was Mama Darden who finally spoke.

"Well, I don't believe a word you are saying about that boy," she said calmly and coldly.

Adria shook her head—not so much in surprise, but disappointment.

"Of course you don't. Of course you would take up for him and not me. Of course you would, because in your eyes, their family can do no wrong. I am sick of all of them, I'm sick of you."

"Sit down sweetheart," Papa Darden pleaded, "And lower your voice."

But Adria was done pacifying her parents. The volcano inside her exploded and she heard herself saying a lot about the church and the leaders and members and whatever else would come to her mouth. The discomfort in her heart settled in her stomach and she felt her whole body was about to erupt. She placed both hands over her mouth and ran into the bathroom before she had made another fool of herself. Then she threw up.

Looking back on it now, Adria understood Mama Darden and Papa Darden were only acting out of their experience and they meant well, but at that point in her life, Adria had given all she could and only desired to get away from their way of doing things.

Adria remained unapproachable for the next two days and did not come out of her room except to go to the bathroom. No one disturbed her. Francine left to go spend some time with her friends and her brothers were busy doing their usual activities.

The two days of silence were enough for her to plan her next steps. She knew she could no longer live the way she was living. Adria was disappointed and frustrated and knew she would continue withering in this current lifestyle. She could leave. She had her college degree. Adria had been counting on the money in the graduation cards placed in her hands at the ceremony and celebration to start a new life, but even without it, she could find a way to start over.

That night, she could hear Papa Darden and Mama Darden arguing and she knew the conversation concerned the episode at lunch the day before. Adria decided to leave on the next day.

Adria talked to Papa Darden and informed him of her plans of moving in with one of her friends. He was hurt but he indicated that he understood and gave her one of the checks from his personal account to help her. Then he told her to call him in a few days.

Adria looked at her Dad's concerned expression and reassured him, "I'll be fine, and I promise to keep in touch."

Adria called one of her college friends to come and pick her up and then she left quietly out the side door with one suitcase, a backpack, and her purse. She wrote Francine a note; however, she was so distraught, she forgot to leave it on her bed.

Adria sighed heavily when she thought about the words she could remember saying on that day and the things she could not remember vocalizing. It must have been particularly stinging as she and her mother did not talk to each other for three years.

Within six months, she had moved to a different state, was living in a two-bedroom-apartment with some friends and sleeping on their couch. The educated woman with a four-year degree had not planned her life very well. This was *not* what she had envisioned for herself.

During the time she searched for employment, Adria's lifestyle consisted of heavy partying as she tried to make up for all the years when she was not allowed to do anything but go to church. She referred to this time as her 'education of the streets' as her Christian childhood upbringing protected her from the harsh realities of the way a lot of people lived daily.

Adria found work through a temporary agency. She worked during the day and partied at night and all weekends. This behavior continued as long as there was money in the household. But because her hourly wages were not enough to really meet her needs, she often found herself in the place where once the money ran out, there were deep discussions and frantic actions to get additional funding. Even still, Adria was determined to make her life work. She was finally free to celebrate life without any fear and to be herself.

While Adria's group of friends knew all the popular socializing locations, including house, pool parties, clubs, and cook-outs, there was one location that would become a favorite hang-out spot on Saturday evenings. The club was located in a large two-story building with a gazebo, chairs, tables, and benches on the outside. Adria found herself hanging out here most often, even when her friends decided to venture off to another social site. She enjoyed the dancing and music.

One evening, she rocked slowly to the old school soulful sounds of artists such as Aretha Franklin, Xscape, EnVogue, Luther Vandross and the Isleys. The bartender placed a drink in front of her.

"Complements of the house," he stated and walked away. Adria accepted the drink and continued enjoying herself. A few minutes later a man took a seat on an adjacent stool.

"Are you responsible for this drink?" Adria inquired as she looked into the eyes of a well-groomed older man with salt and pepper hair, deep brown eyes, and a slow smile.

"I heard you like wine spritzers," he replied. "My name is J, and this is my club." He reached out his hand.

"Nice to meet you, J," Adria responded with a smile and shook his hand gently.

J asked the usual questions but gave no indication that he had already made some general inquiries about her. Her regular visits to the club on Saturday nights had given him the opportunity to observe her behaviors and learn of her drinking habits.

After a few minutes, J stated he appreciated her patronage and then he left his business card with his personal phone number. Adria then placed her contact information under her middle name 'Dionne' in his list of contacts in his phone, at which he smiled and called her 'Lady Deo.'

Adria's Transformation

And so, their friendship began.

J offered her a job as a waitress, working on weekends and some weeknights. Eventually, though, the work friendship became more personal, and they started dating. But Adria understood the rules of engagement: she was just one of his 'girls', one of the women he was dating, and she was okay with that. She was very fond of him, and he of her, but she was not in love with him. Adria had grown accustomed to keeping people at a distance and this relationship cemented her behavior. So she was willing to accept it for what it was and get what she could out of it.

Because Adria was dependable and discrete, J asked her to accompany him into the room where the money was counted for deposit one day. It was not an issue for her as she had counted money on numerous occasions in her church. Her ability to not be overwhelmed or react to the large sums of money counted positioned her to manage other duties. That was when she gained even more insight into J's multiple revenue streams and started coming into her own. She saved what she made at the club and was finally able to afford her own apartment.

After that, Adria became one of J's favorite girls and often accompanied him to special dinners and gatherings at prominent club members' houses.

Once, they received a birthday invitation from a friend and Adria placed a lot of attention on finding the perfect gift for his friend. She then took the time to meticulously wrap the present. It was beautiful and customized for the recipient. The friend loved it and kept bragging about how they did not want to even open the gifts in the bag. Adria's employment as the 'Queen of Giftwrapping' began as J always had an extra special gift for each of his friends. It was years before Adria realized the extra special 'gifts' J offered were his friends' favorite expensive narcotics. She had now become his assistant in his down-low drug dealing world, which she, at first, had no knowledge of, eventually justified. She felt a pang of guilt regarding 'all of the goodies' but it never lasted long, partly because she knew she was well protected by J. She knew one conversation with the wrong person could change her entire life and land her in jail, but she also understood that J was a master businessman and carefully managed his world. All Adria had to do was find and wrap the perfect birthday gifts. Then, as his girlfriend, accompany him to an awe-inspiring birthday bash.

Everything for her felt methodical and shallow at times, but this was all she was capable of handling. From Adria's perspective, this was the perfect relationship. But that changed quite abruptly one day, when the club had to close its doors and she had to sever her relationship with J.

Adria had shared only a few of these details with Bryson and she wondered how he would react if he knew the whole story. Would he understand what she now did? That she needed the years away from her rural hometown to find not just herself, but to further understand the imperfections of humans and the love of God that never fails, no matter what?

Adria's new experiences after college broadened her horizons to obtain a lot of first-hand knowledge. But the distance also caused her to miss out on many of her family's important interactions. It was a Monday night years later that Adria learned about Gerrard's health challenges from an Auntie. She became fearful and reached out to her brother herself, but she did not discover the truth of his condition until she made an unannounced visit to his home and spent hours conversing. Adria started to connect with him more often. Then received the phone call of his deteriorating health. The medical professionals explained he would soon transition and advised she should come home as quickly as possible. Adria and her family sat in the hospital room and would not leave him. The night he passed, she had become tired and gone down to the cafeteria to get a beverage. When she returned to his room, she could hear the sobs of her family members and knew he had left them.

Adria could feel and 'hear' her heart shattering into a million pieces. She fell on her knees beside the bed, grabbed his hands and begged her brother to come back.

"If you come back, I promise never to leave you again and I will stay right by your side, so no one else can betray or take advantage of you again, I promise, I promise!" She remembered saying. "Please, please, please come back, I am so sorry I left you unprotected, I am so sorry brother, please forgive me!"

Eventually, she and her family were forced to say goodbye. It was the death of Gerrard that jolted Adria to move back to her hometown, and to her traumatized family as quickly as possible after his transition. She no longer desired to live away from them. She wanted to remain close by just in case something like this happened in the future.

Adria's decision not only returned her to her hometown but also to a God who became a major source of comfort and healing to her. And true love... When Adria returned to Rockville, it was certainly NOT her intent to meet someone like Bryson to love, but she did and from the day when she attended the church afternoon service, her life had truly changed.

The feelings for Bryson were new to Adria as she had never previously experienced these types of deep sentiments or this level of emotional or spiritual connection. But this situation with Bryson and Mary had really caused her to do some deep soul searching. The out-of-control feelings Adria was experiencing were way too familiar and she didn't like that. Understanding that, she had booked an appointment with her therapist as soon as she could. But until then, she had to manage.

One thing she understood now was how much God was with her, protecting her and guiding her footsteps. If nothing else, she had to trust that.

Adria's phone rang again. This time, it was her father. She never ignored her father's calls.

"Hello Poppie," Adria answered with a gentle demeaner.

"Hello, Honey Bun," Papa Darden replied. "I am just calling to check in on you."

Adria deeply sighed before answering. "I am doing okay, Poppie, I guess," She continued to look down at the phone as if she could see his face as she spoke.

"Well, I am about five minutes from your home and wanted to stop by and give you a visit. Is that okay?" Papa Darden asked.

"Sure, that's fine!" Adria stated.

"Okay, see you soon!"

Papa Darden arrived at his daughter's front porch within just a few minutes. Adria opened the door and smiled. "Hi there Poppie! I am so glad to see you!"

Papa Darden gave Adria a big hug and then handed her a bag of goodies he purchased.

Adria's Transformation

"How's my girl! I got us a few things just in case you were hungry!"

"Thank you so much!" Adria stated and reached for the large bag full of all kinds of snacks. "Come on, I am hanging out at home today. We can go sit in the screened-in porch if you want."

"Lead the way," he said and followed her. They each took a seat in one of the rockers and placed the bag on the table between them.

"So, are you okay honey bun?" he asked her.

"I was just sitting here thinking about a lot of things, some good memories and some not so good... but yeah, I am okay," Adria replied.

"Our family has been through a lot of situations, and they have been really, really difficult...but God saw us through," he said.

Adria chuckled inwardly at her Poppie as these were the words he always used when he was comforting someone. It was his way of communicating and she accepted it.

"But, I'm not here to talk about the family. I'm here to talk about you. You know we heard about Bryson..."

Adria nodded; her suspicions confirmed. She imagined Francine running around and telling everyone she knew.

"And that Mary is pregnant with his child..."

"That is what we have been told," Adria said, dryly.

"It will be number two for him and he is not married," Papa Darden stated as he looked out into the backyard landscape.

She didn't respond to him.

"Our family's sort of grew up together," Papa Darden said. "We would all worship at the meetings during the year and it was good seeing the young people use those gifts as you were growing up. All of the boys got a lot of attention from the girls, and we watched it. Actually, we tried to keep our eyes on it, but it's hard to be in two places at one time. So, I just had to remind my boys the trouble they could get in. It was up to Mama to train you and your sister and keep you out of trouble." Papa Darden paused momentarily and sighed heavily. "No, this is nothing new, except you all had the opportunities your Mama and I didn't have. You know, to keep it from happening. We just wanted you to take advantage of all of them. We both wished you would experience life a little before you started a family. It worked for some of you and not for all of you. Even though it's nothing new, the way we coped with issues was not the way you young people handle things today. We were in a different time period, and we had a different attitude towards the outcomes."

There was a sound in Papa Darden's voice, the way he talked slowly and deliberately and took extra time with his words, that caused Adria to take notice. She watched as he stretched out his legs and re-adjusted his left pants leg before continuing.

"You know, all of you are my children. No one could deny that. But that first child your mama lost wasn't mine," Papa Darden admitted in a soft voice. "Your Mama was really crazy about this other guy, but he was not the marrying type at all. He just sort of left her to handle everything herself."

"Is that when she met you?" Adria asked.

Papa Darden nodded, his eyes still looking over the backyard.

Adria's Transformation

"I knew her and her family very well, but yes, it was when we got closer. The rejection hurt her, but not as much as being left to have and raise that child on her own. So, she and I got married. Then about a month later she lost the baby."

"Did you love her?" Adria asked.

"I cared for your mother and over time I did learn to love her, but I had another one in my life I had to walk away from," Papa Darden confessed. "It was much harder than I thought it would be, as you just can't stop caring for someone overnight and they had different personalities. But I knew I did the right thing. Especially when you all started coming along. All of my children and grandchildren bring me so much joy!"

Adria reached over and laid her hand on her Poppie's hand for comfort. No one doubted how much he loved his family. He showed it every single day. He turned to Adria before continuing.

"When you left, it affected her. She could always count on you and for the first time ever, you were not there for her. Mama always thought you would come back within a few months once you cooled off. But you didn't. I blamed her for pushing you too hard and blamed myself for letting her."

He paused again, but this time, he picked up the snack bag and started going through it, as if it was the most logical thing to do, and it would lessen the impact of what he had to say. He picked out his favorite snack and continued speaking.

"Your Mom, well, in some ways she will never change, but I believe she means well. And I also believe she wants her children to be happy. She has not talked a lot about your situation, but I think she might be a little afraid for her oldest daughter, especially since you are so much in love with this guy." Papa Darden looked at her. "She never wanted you girls to be in the place she was in." He grabbed her hand and held it. "But we will get through this," Papa Darden finished. "With God's help, we will get through this!"

Adria sighed and squeezed his hand, speechlessly trying to process all of what had just been communicated with her.

That afternoon, after her father left, Adria's phone rang. This time, it was Bryson requesting a video call. She accepted it.

"Hi there," Bryson stated, though Adria noticed he looked solemn and tired. He was walking down the hall to the main sanctuary.

"Hi," Adria answered. "How are you?"

"I am in between rehearsals and thought about you as the chorale practice was starting soon. I had a song in mind, and I wanted you to be the lead vocalist. It's a ballad and I think it would be great if you would start learning it," Bryson said waited for her reaction to his request.

Adria could feel her heart start beating harder. She didn't remove her gaze from the phone but continued to stare at Bryson. "Let me think about it. I was contemplating taking some time off from the choir," Adria paused for a second, "But I am just not sure right now."

Adria watched as Bryson tried to keep a supportive face on. He stopped before going further.

"Well, I hope not," Bryson stated, "for a lot of reasons. Your presence is missed."

Adria's Transformation

Adria smiled at his words.

"I will send you the song and call you later. You can let me know if you are willing to sing it. I love you," Bryson said.

"I love you too," Adria quickly responded. Then the video call ended. For a few moments, her life felt normal. That was all she wanted, to get back to the place where she and Bryson were just enjoying being a couple. However, the reality was she and Bryson were facing a major challenge right now. And that was causing her to feel vulnerable and to vacillate between anger and sadness.

Dr. Paula Y. Obie

Chapter 9
Dr. Bailey Truisms

Dr. Bailey's office suite was spacious enough for several comfortable chairs and a large desk. A mahogany wood bookcase along the wall was filled with international artwork. The earth tones were soothing, and there were relaxing, nature sounds used as white noise to help clients unwind. There was ample room for her patients to walk around or pace for a few feet. There was also a small sofa at the corner of the room.

Adria sat in an overstuffed comfortable chair with Dr. Bailey facing her. She had been introduced to her practice by her primary care physician to assist with her mourning process after Gerrard's death. And stayed with her even after she was able to properly grieve, sharing with Dr. Bailey all of the ups and downs of life, including the roller coaster that had become her life with the news of Mary's pregnancy.

"Do you love this guy for real?" Dr. Bailey asked candidly.

"Yes, I love him," Adria responded quickly.

"Do you think he loves you, for real?" Dr. Bailey inquired, "You know, the way Paul described love in I Corinthians 13 and 4?"

Dr. Bailey was a Christian therapist, who believed in the wholistic method of faith, science, and practical living. She often employed the biblical experiences into her therapies to assist with her patients' healing.

Adria looked into Dr. Bailey's eyes, "Yes, I guess so."

"Okay, then, do you trust Bryson?"

"I was really trying," Adria said, her voice raised. "I saw a future for us, you know."

"I'm not here to tell you what to do, Adria. I'm just here to help you work through this. So, tell me, why can't you see a future now?"

"If he is the father of this child, then my issue would be with the mother as she is already a problem," Adria insisted. "A big problem."

"So, it's more about the mother, than the child?" Dr. Bailey probed.

Adria paused briefly. "Yes, I just feel if she was pregnant with Bryson's child, then she would find a way to push me so far out of the picture and make our lives—mostly my life, really hard. I've seen a similar scenario where the mother was just impossible, for no reason. Just because. I don't have problems loving a child, it's not their fault and it's not fair to blame them at all," Adria confessed. "I am just feeling totally selfish right now ...totally, totally selfish."

"And perhaps afraid of losing your man?" Dr. Bailey inquired, pushing Adria just a little further to her truth.

Adria chose not to audibly respond to the question, but rather gave a facial expression to indicate it was a probability.

"Why would you be afraid of losing the man you love and whom you say loves you?"

"I don't know. There is just a lot going on inside of me."

"Ah yes, there is always a battlefield in the mind. We all must overcome!"

Adria raised her eyes and looked directly at Dr. Bailey.

"I don't want someone to be able to come in and destroy my happiness like this. I feel out of control, like I don't matter. And I matter!" She insisted, pointing to herself. Then in a lower volume repeated the statement it as if she were saying it only to herself, "I matter!"

"Yes, you do! But you're the only one who can decide what you want to do. Talk to Bryson. Keep your communication open and honest. When is Mary planning to take the DNA test?" Dr. Bailey asked.

Adria shrugged her shoulders. "I don't know. She hasn't consented to a DNA test yet. It's like she is playing games."

"Hmm...so what do *you* want Adria?" Dr. Bailey inquired.

Adria opened her mouth and shut it. She knew what she wanted, or she thought she did. She said, "If he makes time for me and I can be a priority, rather than an afterthought, then maybe...who knows...at this time...? Anyway...anyways..." Adria was babbling and not articulating her thoughts well, raising her shoulders up and down.

"Well, tell you what. Think about it this week because this is a question you're going to have to answer, not for Bryson, not for Mary but for yourself. You're going to have to figure out what you truly want. This is where you're going to find your voice."

Dr. Bailey looked through her notes, and asked, "How are you sleeping?"

"Okay," Adria said, "The pills have helped a lot. Especially lately. For the longest time, they just sat in my medicine cabinet."

"But they were there when you needed them," Dr. Bailey replied and then glanced at the clock. "I'll contact Dr. Bruce's office for a consult regarding the sleeping pills. He may want you to make an appointment before he renews the prescription. And I'll see you next week, okay?"

Adria nodded her head as she accepted the appointment card. She trusted her therapist, knowing how easy it was to fall into her previous bad habits.

Adria made it through the rest of her day and worked hard to complete her duties. There were days when she was just exhausted from overthinking/obsessing about her circumstances. Adria felt as if someone slammed the *pause* button on her life and she did not have the power to press *play*. Not knowing whether Bryson was the father of Mary's baby and having her anxiety levels all over the place was mentally draining, but what was worse was not knowing if she could handle the situation if it turned out he was. This had her on edge and she had to force herself to focus on one thing at a time...and pray. Praying was what she could do consistently.

Her normal routine had been disrupted and she had not attended a church service in a while. First Lady Becca phoned to check-in a couple of times and left messages stating how much she missed seeing her at church.

Adria knew she needed to return First Lady Becca's phone calls, but she did not have the courage to talk to her. Instead, she sent her a text stating she had a lot going on, including being very busy at work and would see her at church on Sunday—and to keep her in her prayers.

That afternoon, Adria pulled her car into her driveway and just sat in her car to relax her head against the headrest for a few minutes. She was listening to one of her favorite songs and wanted to let the music minister to her and give her hope. When the tune came to an end, Adria gathered her things to go into her home and noticed a car pulling in behind her. She recognized it anywhere and was shocked Bryson had simply shown up at her residence without an invitation. She glanced down at her phone to see if she had missed his call or text message and confirmed he had not communicated with her. Adria was not sure if she was annoyed or flattered and watched as he got out of his car with a bunch of roses in his hand and a solemn look. He walked to the driver's side, and she started the ignition to lower the window.

"Hi there," Bryson said.

"Hi."

"Do you want to go for a ride?"

"Right now?" Adria asked, her eyes squinted.

"Yes. Can you go?"

"Sure."

Adria's instinct was to immediately become defensive as she had been interrupted, and he did not alert her he was coming to see her. But she told herself to relax and remained open to the moment. Adria grabbed her purse and phone and got out of her car.

"Here," Bryson stated gently, handing her the roses. "These are for you!"

"Thank you," Adria smiled, appreciatively. "They are beautiful.

They walked to Bryson's car in silence. Once inside, Adria placed the bouquet on the back seat and then looked more intently at Bryson. "He looks beat," Adria told herself, "Apparently I'm not the only one going without proper sleep."

Bryson backed his car out of the driveway and out of the cul-de-sac without saying a word. He did not reach for Adria's hand, and he did not kiss her. It was weird for them to be at this point where the relationship was strained and neither of them seem to know what to do but just remain silent.

Adria relaxed her head on the head support and closed her eyes. She was past exhausted.

"Are you tired?"

"Yes, it's been a very long day."

"I am beat too, but I wanted to see you," Bryson added.

"How did you know I would not have a problem with you just dropping by, unannounced?" Adria inquired.

"I didn't but it was worth the risk."

Bryson pulled into a nearby family leisure area and backed the car into an available space. He remained quiet as he turned off the ignition, grabbed his phone, opened the driver's door, and got out of the car.

Even though she was tired, Adria was becoming more contented with Bryson's unannounced visit. Other than talking on the phone and brief gatherings, the two of them had not really spent a lot of quality time together. Both were cocooning until their lives were allowed to be taken out of this holding pattern.

Adria and Bryson walked around the park in silence. Every now and then, they glanced at each other, but nothing more was said. Adria noted how they didn't hold

Adria's Transformation

hands either. This spoke volumes to how far they had disconnected. This situation had changed them, and if Adria was being honest, it just did not feel comfortable anymore to hold hands. It was as if neither of them felt like they were allowed to take pleasure in those little things couples enjoy, as if they were no longer a couple.

"Do you want to sit down?" Bryson asked as they approached a sitting area.

Adria nodded. The two relaxed on a nearby bench.

Again, silence. No one was talking. Adria wondered why Bryson would bring her here and not talk.

"I just wanted to see you, that's all," Bryson finally said, as though he had read her mind.

"How have you been, really?" Adria asked softly. She was looking straight ahead but could see him in her peripheral vision.

"I am doing my thing, trying to focus on some musical projects and a little songwriting, but not a lot though," Bryson said. "Church is keeping me pretty busy."

"How are Bishop and First Lady?"

"They are doing fine." Bryson stated, "Asked about you. Miss you in the choir and just being around."

"Oh yeah?" Adria responded, "I am coming to church for the 7:45 a.m. service this Sunday."

"Cool. It will be good to worship with you again and seeing you in the sanctuary," Bryson stated, then added quickly, as though he might lose his nerve otherwise, "Can I ask you a question?"

"Yes."

"Are you going to totally shut down on me?" Bryson questioned.

Adria sighed, not totally surprised by the question. It was what she did, after all.

"I am working hard not to ...," Adria admitted, "But sometimes ..." She paused, thinking about what to say next. "Sometimes, I am just tired of thinking about all of this."

Bryson became quiet again. She could see the emotional turmoil on his face, but she didn't know how to fix that for him. All she knew was that this was not the type of problem to be fixed with dinner and roses. She appreciated the effort, but the truth was, this dilemma could transform their lives forever.

"I know. I just ...I don't know... I just miss us!" Bryson stated emphatically. "Don't you miss us, Adria?"

Adria turned towards Bryson, the man she loved and saw as a part of her forever future—until a few weeks ago and now she was feeling conflicted.

"Yes, I do," Adria replied quietly, but it didn't seem enough. Bryson reached over and grabbed her hand. Then he interlocked their fingers. Adria held on and just remained silent.

Chapter 10
To Be Continued

Carla and Adria met off site at a neighborhood coffee shop for their Monday morning meeting. Carla noticed Adria was smiling when she walked through the doors as she was on her phone. It was a good sign.

"Well, someone seems to be in much better spirits today. How was your weekend?"

"It was pretty good, actually. I went to church and then spent some time with my family afterwards," Adria added and sat down in the chair in front of Carla. "It all helped to lift my spirit."

"So, how are you and Bryson?" Carla asked cheerfully as she placed her hands on the table. She assumed it was Bryson Adria was speaking with when she entered the coffee shop.

"We talk daily, but it's strained. It's really hard for us right now," Adria answered, "but I have decided not to allow it to totally destroy my happiness."

"Sounds wise to me. It's a lot to think about and can be overwhelming."

"Exactly."

"Well, it's good to see you smile and laugh again. I hope this will all be over soon, and you can get on with your love life," Carla added before she turned her attention to the documentation in front of her.

Adria left the table to place her order. Carla noted Adria's phone was ringing, and the person calling was 'Douglas.' Before Adria could return to the table, there was a text, again from 'Douglas.'

Carla did not change her expression, but rather stayed focused on the task at hand. She was aware Adria and Douglas had been friends since they were teenagers, so she did not want to jump to conclusions. Adria was like a sister to her, and Carla needed to make sure, because of this vulnerable space she was in, that Adria was not driving in the wrong direction down a one-way street.

Adria returned with a hot mocha and Danish. Then she flipped over her organizer to review the monthly reports. Her phone illuminated again—another call from Douglas. Carla watched as Adria glanced at the caller ID and pressed the 'Decline' button. Another call followed—it was from Bryson and again, Adria declined it.

Carla worked extremely hard to keep quiet and not interfere as this was none of her business, but she and Adria had grown to be each other's confidants and she just wanted to know what was going on. Carla initiated the conversation.

"I can't wait to see you and Bryson as happy as you were before," Carla offered. "I have really been praying for you two."

"I appreciate it. You know, it's been a tough time for us and frankly, we are both just drained," Adria confessed.

"How is Bryson coping with everything?"

"He looks exhausted, but then this is his fault, so I would expect him to be worried about it," Adria said, matter-of-factly. Carla looked at Adria's face as she spoke, and it shocked her to see her talking about Bryson with a much different tone now. It did not sit well with her.

"Yeah, this is a tough situation to be in, but not so uncommon these days," Carla pressed.

"It doesn't make it right," Adria responded curtly.

"No, but unprotected sex is going to create babies if you are fertile, and some people just take too many chances."

Adria paused before continuing.

"I guess Bryson and I are in a holding pattern until we get the results of the DNA test. If we get one."

"I get it, but then what will happen if he is the father?" Carla asked gently as she looked at Adria, "Will you stop loving him?"

Adria took a bite of her Danish, followed by a sip of her mocha coffee. She didn't seem to want to respond.

"I am sure Mary is banking on the two of you breaking up so she can swoop down and be there for Bryson," Carla cautioned.

"You think so?" Adria asked. "It takes two to make a baby."

"True...so true, but she wants your man. It's no secret!"

Adria was slowly chewing her food. "How do you know she wants my man? Or do you think they were secretly seeing each other, and Bryson just won't admit it to me? Like, maybe he didn't want anyone to know about her?" Adria asked, though it seemed like she was playing games with Carla.

"I don't know, but I would believe Bryson's version of the story before I believe anything Mary says. She has not kept her wishes a secret. She is so head over heels in love with him and has been trying to get his attention for some time now. And he is not the only one, Adria. You have brothers, you know how all this works," Carla shared.

"Look, all I know is that if this child is Bryson's, she will make my life a living hell and harder than I deserve for it to be."

"Yes, but you have Bryson's heart, so he would back her off and put you first and love his child. I can't imagine what he is going through. First, Rheta, now this? Lord, have mercy!"

Adria didn't seem convinced, and said, "Well, men need to be more careful who they sleep with, don't they?"

Carla squinted her eyes at Adria dramatically.

"What?" Adria responded with some annoyance.

"If you throw away what you and Bryson have, you may regret it for the rest of your life. Be careful because it is exactly what she wants!" Carla stated, holding her coffee mug with both hands. She was not in the habit of giving any type of relational advice, but Adria needed her to interject her feelings.

Adria's phone illuminated again, and the caller ID showed Douglas' name.

"And another thing, you know you won't be happy with Douglas for long, because you don't love him in the same way you love Bryson," Carla added.

"We're just friends," Adria said dryly.

"Perhaps, but Douglas is here for you, and I am sure is making you happier than Bryson during this time. He is not Bryson though. Right now, you just have an emotional boyfriend in Douglas and that is a very poor substitute."

Adria's Transformation

Adria listened and nodded her head.

"I just hope the next few weeks are going to give me my life back."

"The Adria I know, can handle this. No matter what happens, don't hand Mary your man on a silver platter. She needs to see this scenario is not going to break you and Bryson apart."

"But it's not easy!" Adria whined.

"I know it's hard. You are going to have to trust more and have greater faith." Carla replied. "Just like he did not marry Rheta, Bryson does not want to get involved with Mary! He wants you."

"Then why did he have a sexual relationship with her?"

"Are you serious right now, Adria?" Carla asked with a quizzical face. She was unconditionally here for her friend, but she was starting to lose patience. "Are you telling me *you* have never had a sexual relationship? Wake up. That's just the way things are right now," she said, and because she thought she might have come off too strong, she added, "I am on your side, Adria!"

"Okay," Adria responded. It was a hard truth, but it was truth, nonetheless. Sensing there was nothing else she could say to help Adria, Carla returned her attention to the reports on the company's quarterly financial data in front of her.

Once the off-site meeting adjourned, the two businesswomen returned to the office, located just a few blocks down the street. They worked throughout the day, keeping their attention at the tasks at hand and business obligations, even ordering dinner when the day grew late. When the food came, Carla and Adria relaxed a little and enjoyed their cuisines. At one point, Carla noticed that

Adria made it a point to turn her phone over, so that when it rang or a text or notification was received, it would not disturb them. She wanted to keep the conversation from earlier going but opted to keep the focus on work.

"I am happy with where we are with these assignments," Carla announced. "These types of days always remind me of the times when we first met and worked together. Do you remember those road trips, the fancy hotels and meals?"

Adria nodded.

"Those were good days." She sighed, placed down her fork and said, "I am truly full. Can we continue this on tomorrow?"

Carla could see she was feeling the effects of the delectable meal and was getting sleepy. Actually, they both were and if Carla was being honest, she was in no mood for work and was ready to drive home, take a long, hot shower and relax into her amazingly comfortable bed.

"Yes, I think all of this can wait until tomorrow," Carla confirmed. "This meal was certainly on point, and I am getting tired too."

But even with that said, Carla felt the urge to revisit Adria's personal scenario again. She wanted to know Adria was going to be alright.

"Adria, you know I love you and you are my girl."

"I know."

"I am concerned about you in a big way. You've worked hard to get where you are. And I'm not trying to tell you what you need to do, I just ... I just want to make sure you're not throwing that relationship away," Carla said plainly.

"You are correct, I have worked hard, and I never anticipated being in love," Adria said. "But that's where

I am now. I came home to heal, and I found Bryson and now all this...?" Though her emotions had threatened to get the best of her again, Adria simply let it go and stared at her cup.

"What do you want to do, Adria?" Carla asked. "You two love each other."

"Yes, we do, but I am just not prepared emotionally for this type of craziness."

"Craziness?" Carla asked, incredulously.

Adria looked up at Carla as though she had said something wrong.

"Yes, he and Mary created this craziness for me." Adria stated.

Carla repeated the question.

"So, what are you going to do?"

Adria pushed the swivel chair away from the table, stood, picked up her finished plate and other food trash and walked to place it in the waste can. She then returned to the chair and sat down. Her facial expression and body language offered insight to her true feelings and her raw emotions. Carla wanted to fix all Adria's problems, but she knew she couldn't. She had to let Adria do that. She watched as her friend opened her mouth and began to speak what was in the deepest recesses of her heart.

"Carla, this is the first time I have ever felt anything more than just shallowness or fondness for anyone. I didn't even think I could ever feel this way, especially after what happened in college," Adria admitted.

"What happened in college?" Carla asked with a furrowed brow and a frown.

"It's not important now, let's just say I remained focused on school and on trying to have a good life. But now there is this uncontrollable issue."

"But you know life is full of uncontrollable problems," Carla stated softly.

"Ugh!" Adria yelled loudly. "I am so sick and tired of other people's problems impacting and taking away from me, Carla. I am just sick of it...so sick of it! I didn't come home for this, at all!"

"No, but you can't just throw true love away either, just because it's tough, or inconvenient," Carla responded.

Adria stood up again and began to walk around.

"I don't want to throw it away...I just don't want my life evolving around anyone else's decision. When I was growing up, my whole life revolved around what others needed or wanted me to do! I guess I was just too nice, and my Mom loved to boss me around. Leaving home gave me the opportunity to get away and learn more about myself and just grow up. It also made me realize that this is my life too and I promised myself to try to make it as fulfilling as possible."

Adria stopped walking and turned to Carla.

"Say Bryson is the father of this child. I am convinced he loves me and not her. And I am convinced he will love the child. *But...*" Adria stopped pacing for a moment, as if she were speaking to a client, "But then I would have to deal with the child's mother, forever."

"But what if he is not the father of the child, Adria? Then if you walk away from it all, you will break your heart!" Carla stated deliberately. "Can you live with that?"

"It would be really, really hard...," Adria confessed and let her voice trail off.

"I know you are scared, Adria!" Carla acknowledged. "And frustrated and angry and just a wee bit self-righteous, right? But you can't keep putting this off. You have to move forward."

"I want to move on!" Adria stated sincerely.

"With or without Bryson?' Carla questioned her pointedly and made a face. "I thought you said you loved him."

Adria stopped cold and looked at Carla. "I do love Bryson!"

"Then prove it!" Carla stated emphatically. "Prove it!"

"What does everyone want from me? I am not the source of the problem here at all! For some reason, people expect me to be the one who can handle anything." Adria sat down in her chair. "I just don't want to accept things for the sake of accepting them when they are not going to always benefit me!"

"It's either you want Bryson, or you don't!" Carla stated. "To me, it's just that simple!"

"You are asking me to just accept all of this baggage?" Adria argued.

"I am asking you to decide what kind of love you have for this man and then move on with your plans," Carla responded. "I'm not trying to tell you to just accept Bryson. I'm saying, take control of your life!"

Adria stood up and walked around the table and pulled out the chair beside Carla, sat down in the seat and just glared at her. Carla could tell she had hit every nerve ending in Adria's body. And Carla understood, if it had been anyone else besides her, Adria would have become angrier and tuned her out long ago. As such, this offered Carla the opportunity to speak into Adria's life and that's what she did.

"You will have to decide what *you* want Adria!" Carla offered purposely. Then she pointed her finger at her, "Look out for your dreams!" Carla then reached over and picked up her trash from their dinner and walked to the waste basket. She returned to her chair, satisfied that everything that needed to be said had been said and was ready to go home. She gazed at Adria who remained in her chair. She eventually nodded her head and looking up at the ceiling, finally said, "You are right."

☙

Adria's cell phone rang several times during the dinner, and she received ongoing texts. Adria reached down to pick up her phone to further review the list of calls. There was one call each from Bryson and Douglas, one text each from Mama Darden, Francine, Bryson, and Douglas. There was no call from Poppie, so there must be no real issues going on in the Darden household.

It was Adria's routine to return calls with her immediate family during the ride home. Although tonight she wanted to return the calls, she decided against it and embraced the silence to engage in deep thinking during her twenty-minute commute. Carla's words were spinning around in her head as she drove with no music... and just her thoughts.

A few weeks earlier, Adria and Bryson would talk several times during the day, and it was not a problem as their love was one of the greatest highlights of her life. Their love made her feel whole and she was finally able to experience something other than shallowness.

Adria was stunned to have these types of problems so soon in the new relationship and there was so much at stake. She resisted daily the urge to return to her former self and run away from the problems or perform emotional and mental disappearing acts.

But the truth was, she was doing that in her indecisiveness. She needed to make a decision. The man she saw in her future as her husband, and the father of her children, had so many of the characteristics for which she had been praying. Bryson had a lot to offer, but he also had a lot of baggage.

Then again, so did Adria. The truth is they both had issues. The only difference was that a lot of Bryson's life experiences were out in the open!

Daily, Adria was unraveling emotionally as she was not sure she had enough courage to deal with this type of situation. Douglas became the only constant person in her life who did not bring her extra troubles and issues and she was truly grateful. But she knew Carla was right when she spoke the truth about how she was esteeming him. Carla became an even greater friend tonight.

In a matter of weeks, her very happy life had turned into a world of confusion, and she was not in the mood for this type of drama. Her heart was trying to make decisions for her and then her mind was constantly interfering with the process. The battle was wreaking havoc on her mentally and emotionally.

Adria admitted silently Carla was on point with her observations and priority list. Adria needed to take control and make key decisions to become more empowered. So, tonight she was going to decide about her future, and let Bryson know her decision.

Prior to taking the exit to direct her towards her neighborhood, Adria had one more thought. She needed to talk to Francine, and she wanted to talk to her tonight!

Adria turned into Francine and Craig's street and parked her car on the curb. She could hear music in the back of the house and could smell the grilled food. She walked down the driveway and into the backyard and shouted, "Hello."

"Auntie A!?" Her nieces, Kazya and Krystal, screamed and ran into the arms of their aunt. Her nephew, Zedrick, jumped up from his chair and also gave her a big hug.

Francine and her husband Craig were sitting at the outdoor table eating, relaxing, enjoying the music and the family.

"Hey Sis!" Craig stated cheerfully, "You are just in time for the food, right off the grill! Come on up and grab you a plate."

Francine looked up and saw the look on Adria's face and said, "Hey girl, what are you up to? Are you hungry?" Francine's plate was filled with barbecue chicken, corn on the cob and grilled veggies.

"I am not hungry, I just wanted to stop by and see you all," Adria said. She retrieved a beverage from the cooler on the porch and then sat down at the table. "I saw where you had called me earlier."

"I was just checking in on you." Francine offered, "I talked to Mama, and she was worried about you."

Adria nodded. She opened her drink and took a sip.

"Whew, what a day!" Adria declared.

"What's going on?" Craig asked. "You look a little beat down. Do you need something a little stronger in a cup?"

Adria laughed aloud. "I just might! But no, this soft drink works fine."

Adria's Transformation

"We got you covered," Craig laughed. "Just check out the cooler. In the meantime..." Craig got up from the table and ushered his children into the yard to give the sisters some privacy. "...we'll let you talk."

After he had walked away from the table, Francine inquired, "So, what's up, Sis?"

"I am just trying to wrap my head around my life, and it's not been easy!" Adria confessed. "I have had a lot of epiphanies and reality checks today."

"Oh yeah? So, what are you going to do? Did you decide that?" Francine asked. "How are you going to handle it?"

Adria sighed heavily, while looking at the beautiful landscape around them. "It's hard to believe how much my life has changed in these past few weeks. It's unbelievable to me, how all of this has just all blown up in my face. It's just simply unreal! Thinking about the next steps has been on my mind twenty-four seven and it's consuming me."

"Well, I told you he slept with a lot of women in the church and Mary was just one of them!" Francine reiterated.

"Yes, you did, Sis, but something way down on the inside is just really bothering me about this whole situation." Adria said, looking down at her beverage, then back at Francine before continuing. "I just can't put my finger on it, but something is just not adding up," Adria stated.

"Or is it you just do not want to accept the fact Bryson is a womanizer!" Francine offered.

"Oh, I accept the fact that he's had sex with more than one woman and *yes* it *did* make him a womanizer," Adria said, still looking at her sister, "but why have the other women not come forward to complain about him, if he indeed was as bad as you say he is? Maybe, maybe they just enjoyed being with him!"

Francine picked up a piece of her barbecue chicken and took a bite before speaking. She looked at Adria and said, "How do you know they have not complained?"

"Because I feel if there had been a lot of complaints about him sleeping with every woman in the church then Bishop and the church board would have had to get rid of him before now," Adria replied, her eyes on Francine.

"Maybe they just were more focused on the fact he is a good musician, packed the church out every Sunday and it was more important to everybody," Francine offered.

Adria smiled gently. "You could be right. The church might be protecting him, as the music department is top notch," Adria responded stoically as she reflected on the music ministry. "However, there's one more thing…well, maybe two more things that don't add up. *Why* did Mary wait until Bryson, and I were a couple to tell him about the baby?"

Francine continued eating her food and drinking her beverage as Adria stared at her sister. Francine remained silent and just shrugged her shoulders in response. When they locked eyes, Adria squinted and frowned.

"*Why* has she not consented to take the DNA test? Trust me, if he was the only guy I was sleeping with, and I was pregnant, then it would have been a no-brainer for me"—Adria pointed to herself—"to consent to the paternity test as soon as I could, just to expose him for the person he is! It would have been my pleasure to get to the truth, so what is the hold up?"

Adria's Transformation

Francine continued to listen to her sister and did not respond. It didn't seem like she was prepared for Adria's line of questioning. Even still, Francine crossed her arms as her agitation began to show.

"I don't know what games you and Mary are playing, and I don't need to know. You may have figured since I walked away from a lot of factors in my life, including my family, that I would walk away from this. I have also allowed a lot of people to just take and take whatever they wanted from me, and I kept turning the other cheek. However, I am no longer *that* Adria! I buried her with Gerrard. I am never walking away from my challenges again. Not without a good fight! I am going to face this one head on! And you can tell Mary exactly what I just said."

Adria glared at her sister and then as she fought back tears, she said, "I am going to go home now as I have had a long day! Thanks for the cold beverage. Tell Craig and the kids I will see them soon."

Adria finished her bold statement and then walked down the steps, along the driveway and got into her car. She remained focused as she drove home, tears rolling down her face as she realized the cruel games women play. To think that her own sister would conspire with a friend just to get her out of the picture. Mary could have easily consented to take the paternity test at the onset of this scenario but refused to do so for some reason. Adria was done waiting on her. She had had enough of being a pawn in this emotional chess game.

"Checkmate!" Adria cried aloud, using her hand to wipe away her tears.

And with that, she decided she was going to remain by Bryson's side no matter what. She prayed their love would be strong enough to see them through this crisis.

Chapter 11
No Longer A Hostage

"Why do you keep asking me to have a DNA test?" Mary cried in the phone. "I told you already, numerous times, it is your child."

"Then you should have no problems confirming it with the paternity test," Bryson stated calmly as he sat in his church office. "I told you; I'll pay for everything."

"You insinuating I am a liar, Bryson Kenton? Like I have said before, you were there, and you and I were intimate. It was six months ago. How much more proof do you need?" Mary insisted.

"I don't understand why there would be a problem if I was the only one you were sleeping with," Bryson stated calmly.

"Those tests aren't safe—"

"They are. Just do a little research—"

"You want me to put my life on the line? You can't make me."

Bryson sighed and quietly said, "I just want to be sure."

The phone went silent.

Bryson and Mary's telephone conversations were becoming predictable. Each week he called her to try and persuade her to consent to have the DNA test. Then Mary would hang up on him only to call again on his cell phone and in his office to discuss the subject repeatedly. Her responses and reactions were the same. She threatened to write a letter to the church board, to call his family, etc. Each time they talked; she was more rigid than in the previous conversation.

This was their routine and it never ended well.

Within a few minutes, the office phone rang again. Bryson looked at the caller ID, expecting it to be Mary. It was Mary's mother. He didn't pick up but waited to hear what message she would leave this time. When Bryson checked the voice mail, she stated how shameful it was for him to act this way towards his unborn child and her daughter.

After today's calls, Bryson felt even more defeated. He had grown tired of waiting. He picked up his cell phone and called his sister Tara.

"Hello there, Brother!" Tara stated. "How are you?"

"Taking it day by day."

"That's all you can do. How's the situation with Mary?"

"No matter what I say, I cannot convince her to take the paternity test and I need to move forward. I'm done trying to get her to change her mind. Can you send me the contact info of the family lawyer referral? I am prepared to pay for everything, including the lawyer fees."

"When was the last time you tried talking to her?" Tara questioned. He could hear the concern in her voice

Adria's Transformation

and knew it likely stemmed from the cost he was willing to incur in this matter just to be done.

"I just got off the phone with her and she refused to take the test, stating I cannot make her. Then her mother called me and left a message saying I ought to be ashamed of myself," Bryson stated. "I am not making any progress at all, and I am ready to know for sure if I am the father!!"

"I will text you the name now," Tara stated. "Give him a call today and then check in with me later!"

"Thanks, Sis," Bryson said and hung up.

At that moment, there was a knock at the office door.

"Come in," Bryson announced.

Bishop walked into the office.

"Hello Minister Bryson. I am just checking in on you."

In their initial visit Bishop gave Bryson spiritual guidance, fatherly advice and then finally an ultimatum—with a definitive timeframe. With each weekly status report, Bryson reassured Bishop he would convince Mary to have a DNA test, however, the progress was not moving as quickly as either of them desired. The church board was also awaiting a response from Bishop regarding how they would proceed as Bryson's contract renewal date was in the near future. And Bishop had not made a recommendation for Bryson to receive a new contract, not yet.

For Bryson though, he had already decided: if he was the father of Mary's unborn child, he would resign from his position as Minister of Music, as he was *not* going to marry a woman he did *not* love. He even started searching for job opportunities in and out of the state. It was going to be difficult, but he was determined to be a good father, and prayed Adria remained by his side. His mind was set. This was the plan to be implemented.

When Bryson provided the latest status regarding Mary's continued reaction, Bishop sat in the chair in front of Bryson's desk.

"Son, I am confused. If I were in her situation, I would have agreed to it weeks ago. I would think it would be the proof she needed to make sure there is no doubt you are the father. Then you could both move on with your lives."

Bryson shrugged his shoulders. "I get the same response each time I make this request. I am just thinking the only way to get this accomplished is for me to hire a lawyer."

Bishop frowned and stood up from the chair.

"This should never have been this complicated," he said. "The woman's protest indicates she has something to hide, but we can't make that judgment."

Bryson shook his head.

"I agree. Maybe she's not certain of who could be the baby's father. Or she just wants to draw out the scenario as it is giving her the attention she seeks."

"Perhaps," Bishop said thoughtfully, "Unfortunately, this is not an atypical scenario, especially if she was upset and hurt the relationship had ended."

Bryson didn't respond, as he was well aware of these type of responses from personal experience.

"You know I usually hesitate to get involved with these types of situations, other than to provide spiritual guidance. You and I have talked, and your options have been clearly stated. I know you well enough to know you're ready to move on to keep the church from being involved in this type of scandal. And I appreciate the

Adria's Transformation

growth and maturity in that. Just don't get discouraged. And don't make any rash decisions. All things will work out the way they're supposed to."

Bryson was humbled by the faith Bishop had in him, and quietly thanked him. Then Bishop stood up and exited his office.

At the onset of this dilemma, Bryson decided the only thing he could do was focus his attention on his job and provide an elevated level of excellence in service offerings. Every rehearsal was orchestrated professionally, and he was well prepared. He worked diligently to remain upbeat, and he was determined not to allow himself to show any signs of deterioration in attitude. Some days were easier than others.

But what he could not control was his relationship with Adria. The weeks since the first conversation about the pregnancy and the DNA testing weighed heavily on each of them. They still communicated daily; however, since the news, the conversations at times seemed hollow and distant.

Bryson was convinced Adria still loved him; however, the longer it took for Mary to agree to a DNA test, the harder it was for him and Adria to talk about anything significant or make future plans. And that was making him worry.

Another important stressor to Bryson's situation was his decision not to discuss this scenario with his parents. He wanted to wait until he had proof he was the baby's father. Truthfully, Bryson was hoping he would not have to reveal this scenario to them at all, but the longer he waited though, the worse he felt.

His sister Tara was the only family member who knew what Bryson was going through. He had asked her not to discuss this with their family and she obliged, but she nonetheless kept encouraging Bryson to give them a heads up and to prepare them for how this situation could impact their lives.

The day finally came when Bryson could not contain his secret any longer. Bryson's discussion with his Mom went as expected: she was furious and lectured her son about fornication, marriage, and any other subject she could think of. Her points were hard and noted. Mama Kenton always defended and rescued her son, but she was growing tired and weary of this task.

"Bryson, it's wrong. If you are the father, then you are going to marry that girl." She spoke passionately. "This has got to stop!"

Bryson's father then talked to him again about the responsibility of thinking with the right part of his anatomy.

Bryson knew his Mom and his Dad were both very proud of him in so many ways, but his weakness caused them unnecessary heartache. All of them remembered the problems they had with Duane's mother, Rheta. The Kenton's fell head over heels in love with Duane and wanted things to work out between the couple, but then the relationship became increasingly complicated, and Bryson had to announce that marriage was out of the question. This led the Kenton's to worry about whether Rheta would allow them to have a relationship with Duane. So far she always welcomed them into his life, but no one in the Kenton household was willing to go through that type of pain again.

After leaving the church, Bryson decided a good run was the only way to clear his head and find some synergy, mentally and physically. He drove to the nearest high school's track, took his running shoes and running attire out of the trunk of the car and prepared himself for his exercise.

As he slowly began the first lap, he could feel his muscles and nerves responding to the process. The stretch prepared his body, and his sheer will ignited his mind for this activity. He usually limited his running to the treadmill, but today Bryson needed to connect with the elements. He needed to sweat, to get toxins out of his system and feel the wind on his face.

As he ran, the sweat poured out of his body like water. Each drop was a cleansing process and was long overdue for his mortal being. He was not running just for his health; he was running to cleanse himself from the need to be surrounded by needy women.

Why was he always attracted to these types of women? Was it because of their responsiveness to him? They poured on him unwavering attention which fed his ego.

Oh, but wait, Adria was not needy, so he could not include her in this category. It was the first time he did not have a thirsty woman in his life. It seemed as soon as he got himself together and tried to do right, there was a major problem. During the second lap, he thought about the night when he went to Mary's house, and they ended up sleeping together. It was in February, the week after Valentine's Day. He remembered the date so well because he did not have someone special on Valentine's Day and was feeling a bit sorry for himself. Mary had fed his ego and earned a place in his bed. But it wasn't what he wanted. All the girls he had dated in the past few years were able to past the 'friend' test, but he wanted to have someone who was more than a friend. Bryson was ready to settle down with a loving wife and have kids together, take vacations, and do all the other things involved with living the family life he always desired.

He rounded the second curve of the track field when he started to count the months from February to today. This was about six months which realistically indicates he could indeed be the father as it was in the timeline when they were together.

Bryson moved into the third lap and during this round he thought about when he and Adria connected. After she came up to Bryson to introduce herself, he was astonished to see the familiar face as it had been years since they were in the same place together. Their friendship was kindled, and he immediately began encouraging her to use her gifts in the music ministry.

For Bryson, he was persuaded he was in love with her singing voice before he was in love with her. For weeks, he just kept saying it was her voice and her anointing which caused him to have that 'feeling' but he soon had to admit it was much more.

He smiled gently as he remembered the moment, he vocalized and embraced the fact he had fallen for her. It was a good feeling and so safe. He did not have a need to rush anything.

"Just one more lap," he told himself. He thought about his son and how he became a father. He and Rheta were dating and grew to be serious about each other. He loved her and had asked her to marry him. She was smart, pretty, and very attentive to his needs. She could be a little jealous at times, but it was not unbearable.

When Rheta became pregnant, she changed completely. She was extremely moody, even more bossy and over-controlling. Everyone blamed the change on hormones, but Bryson provided her support throughout the pregnancy and prepared himself to be both a good father and a husband. He thought it would be best to wait until the baby was born before they got married, hoping Rheta would go back to who she was, but her personality never improved. By the end of the pregnancy, Bryson had become a robot. He was trying to be a perfect person and make sure he made up for not becoming a husband before being a dad, but that changed when his son was born. No one prepared him for the immediate love he had for Duane.

From the minute he saw his head crowning to the time he first held him in his arms, Bryson was in love. He absolutely adored Duane and was ecstatic God blessed him with his son. Understanding that he had to be his best self for Duane, and that he could not do that with Rheta, he broke off not just the engagement, but their relationship. The decision not to marry Rheta was not a surprise to his family, however it caused the type of complications that accompany this kind of choice. That was four years ago. Now he was in the same kind of trouble with Mary and on the verge of losing Adria, even though he had not given into the sexual feelings he felt for Adria.

"Why, God, is it that when you are trying to do good evil is always lurking around?" Bryson knew God was merciful, but he did not know if he had used all his chances at this point.

Bryson took a deep breath as he finished his run. It had revitalized and detoxed him. His objective was to go home, shower and prepare the music for the upcoming week. It was important for him to focus on his church duties and trust God to work out the other details. It was

Tuesday night, and he had the normal number of tasks due on Pastor's desk by Thursday.

As Bryson proceeded down the freeway, and listened to the first track on his playlist, he admitted to himself how much he loved his job as the Minister of Music at GFCC. It was the most fulfilling position he had been blessed to hold. Bishop and First Lady's support empowered him to raise the bar on his individual and church goals. Within the past three years, the music department improved tremendously under his leadership. This position was truly a dream come true. Yet, Bryson knew he had not done enough to protect his blessings.

Bryson arrived at his home and embraced the sanctity it provided. He showered and changed into comfortable clothing. Now he needed to relax his mind, eat some food and possibly get in a better mood before he communicated with Adria later.

Then Bryson's phone rang. It was James, his bass player, calling.

"Hello James," he said.

"Bryson, man, how are you doing?"

"I am doing great. What's up?"

"I have some music I'd like to turn you onto if you have a minute. It's something I have been actually saving for you and wondered if tonight was a good time for you to hear it."

Bryson looked at his watch and although he had other plans, remembered his responsibilities included motivating the creative talents and gifts of others.

"Sure, why don't you come on over and we'll see what you have been working on," offered Bryson.

When James walked in a little while later, he gave Bryson the 'brother's hug'.

Adria's Transformation

"What's up, Big James?" Bryson asked as he showed him in.

"Just a little something-something I have been working on," James reported as he handed Bryson a CD.

"Come on, let's check it out," Bryson stated as he walked into the home studio and inserted his friend's music into his CD player. James took a seat and sat back in anticipation. Bryson played the first track and offered his opinion. Then he played the next two tracks and again shared his immediate thoughts.

"James, these are good tracks. When did you start writing music? I never knew you were a song writer," Bryson inquired.

James tilted his head to one side. "I got inspired one day and I just kept working on it. When I felt comfortable with it, I started laying down the tracks and here we are!"

"Really?" Bryson responded excitedly.

"Yep, I could just hear the music in my head, and I wanted to see how far I could take it." James smiled broadly as he told the story. "And you know I had to put my bestest foot forward before I gave it to you."

"Hey man, this is great! I do have some suggestions, but only a few," Bryson added. "Maybe we can work on it together in the very near future. I am excited."

"Thank you! It means a lot coming from you!"

Bryson removed the CD and gave it to James.

James took the CD and placed it back in its protective covering. He looked as though he had something further he wanted to say.

"Listen, I heard a rumor and I wanted to know if it was true. You don't have to tell me, but I wanted to hear it from you."

"What did you hear?" Bryson inquired.

"I heard Mary is going to have your baby," James responded.

Bryson looked at James and dropped his head before speaking. Then he raised his eyes and spoke.

"That's what she tells me," Bryson reported.

"I didn't know you two were dating." James commented.

"Man, we only got that close once and I protected myself. It was one of those things that was not planned, way before Adria and I started dating. Things went too far," Bryson admitted.

James leaned forward in his seat, his arms resting on both legs. He nodded his head.

"She also told me she was not sleeping with anyone else during that time, so I must be the father," Bryson finished.

"Do you believe her?"

"I don't know. I guess. But I did ask for a DNA test. Her answer has been 'no'. It has been weeks and I have not yet convinced her to take the test," Bryson stated. "Don't you think it's a little strange?"

James continued to listen intently as he spoke, then took a deep breath and said, "Bryson, you have been a good friend to me. Ever since you joined this church, you have encouraged me to use my talent. You believed in me when I didn't believe in myself and helped me move to the next level."

"What you don't know is I was involved with someone earlier this year, who was in love with you." James revealed. "She talked about you a lot as she spent time with me. We started seeing each other regularly, but I knew she wished it were you instead of me."

Bryson stared at his friend and fellow musician.

Adria's Transformation

"I accepted where we were and felt that over time, she would learn to care for me, and she did care *some*, but I knew I was being used," James admitted. "I was just a substitute."

"That's too bad man."

"The young lady was Mary and starting a few months ago we were a *real* couple, if you know what I mean. As a matter of fact, we have been off and on most of this year," James shared. "When I heard she was pregnant, I just assumed the child was mine, but then she tells me she was sleeping with someone other than me. I prayed about it and asked God what to do."

Bryson leaned his head back into his hands and interlocked his fingers, almost in shock.

"Truthfully, Bryson, I am glad you are asking for a DNA test, because I feel very strongly that unless she was sleeping with someone else other than the two of us, the child is mine."

Bryson remained silent and stilled, unsure of how to react.

"Man, I really love her and will take care of her and the child, but she didn't want anyone to know we were dating. Well, I don't know if you can call it dating... I was there whenever she contacted me. It's what she wanted, and I didn't have a problem with it."

James sighed.

Bryson leaned forward before speaking. "James, she told me on more than one occasion I was the only one she slept with then ... as she was celibate and was just very vulnerable only on that day."

"I know what she said, but it was not the truth. I couldn't let you lose everything you have worked for because of a lie," James stated. "Some guys were discussing you at an event I attended, stating they heard you had gotten Mary pregnant. I was a little bit confused but knew she was prone to telling things the way she wanted them to be, so I called her, but she didn't answer," James confessed.

"And this is the woman you fell in love with?" Bryson asked, his tone incredulous. He was concerned now for James, as he understood what it was like to deal with ... dramatic women.

James looked down, almost as if he was ashamed. "She's not a bad person. I think deep down inside Mary is just looking for someone to love and accept her unconditionally."

"So, you met at GFCC?" Bryson asked after a moment. He realized how true James' emotions were and didn't want to dismiss them so easily.

"Yes, we first met at the church festival," James stated, "Then we both showed up at other events and began chatting. Eventually, we exchanged phone numbers."

Bryson then thought about Adria. She had been patient through all of this, but he knew she was getting weary, and their future was contingent upon the results of the DNA.

"James, I owe you. I owe you! You may have just saved my relationship, my future marriage and my children, my life ... my sanity. ... my job... But..." Bryson reached out and gave him a firm handshake that turned into a brother's hug. This was still weighing heavy on his mind, though. "But James, are you sure you want to continue with this woman? She seems to be a lot of trouble."

"One day, I think I can do better and then the next I think I can't!" James responded. "Whenever I pull back, then she showers me with extra attention, and I think maybe I am just the kind of guy she needs."

As much as Bryson wanted to convince James otherwise, to tell him he deserved better, to make it his business to introduce him to women who had a lot going for them, other than playing games, Bryson didn't think he could. There was something about the way James felt for Mary that gave him pause. Was it any different than when Adria walked into his life, and they started dating? Things changed for him and he began thinking differently about his future.

But Adria wasn't Mary, and she hadn't used a pregnancy to try to trap him. And if this was James' child, then James would now have to be the one to deal with Mary for the rest of his life.

Bryson thought about those words, about the possibility that James was the father of Mary's child. This was the best news he had heard in what seemed like an eternity. The crisis *was* not over, but Bryson was now putting all of his faith and positive thinking into James being the child's father.

"You want to grab something to eat? I'm starving," he asked his friend.

James nodded. They exited the house, jumped into Bryson's car and drove to a nearby pizza place. During the meal, Bryson decided to talk to James about his earlier thoughts and encouraged him to proceed cautiously if he intended to continue being with Mary. The promise that Bryson would introduce him to better caliber women was something James could look forward to, if that's what he wanted.

"I have a question for you, Bryson," James stated. "Is it true nice guys like me always get the same type of girl? I mean, we've been talking about a lot of things in our Men's fellowship, including this and it has been giving me a lot to think about, but I wanted your opinion."

"I think there is a possibility we can be too nice," Bryson stated. "People then take advantage of our kindness. And once we show our weaknesses, then they exploit us."

"I see," James stated. "So, how do we change?"

"Personally, I think the change comes when we know *our* worth and what we bring to the table. Then we look out for ourselves more and it helps us make better decisions. I am not an expert though and believe me, I have made a lot of mistakes."

The two continued talking and eventually played a few rounds of pool.

When they parted ways that evening, Bryson was eternally grateful to God and to James. He wanted to share this news with Adria but thought it was better if he waited for the paternity test results.

He also thought about James and wondered if he had given him the type of support he needed today. There was a probability that he was going to be a father, in love someone who did not love him in the same way. Bryson's prayer was that James would find the courage to make the right choices and to look out for himself.

As Bryson finalized all his musical church tasks, he sat quietly in the chair in his living room. This day had been one of those roller-coaster rides where he was forced to take a really hard look at his life. He never anticipated having this conversation with James. But at the same time, the fact that he did not know Mary's true character unnerved him. This behavior represented his life when he was in his twenties. There were times in his past that he did not hang around long enough to learn the true personality or qualities of the woman he was seeing.

Once he started interacting with a female, and then very soon thereafter, she began to vocalize her love for him, well, he had decisions to make. He also realized he was very analytical and would therefore become bored quickly with just one woman, especially, if the woman had few experiences with minimal zeal for life.

Bryson admitted he was not as concerned about a woman's true feelings as he heard the words "I love you" a lot of times. Did he somehow become anesthetized to these words?

He was now in his thirties and sought to learn from his younger self. Three years ago, he accepted a promotion to Minister of Music and was catapulted into a more mature and grown-up world. He was forced to grow from being just a musician to someone who carried the word of God in Music. This was a totally different level of responsibility he was obliged to fully understand. He promised the board of GFCC his relationship with God grew to the point where he was no longer careless with his interactions. Then he was tested and failed. His reputation as a womanizer became serious and challenged his role as a Minister of Music.

Bryson thought about his relationship with God and how grateful he was to have Him open so many doors. He was a born-again Christian, but like other Christians, he had some issues he needed to face. In his situation, his problems evolved around commitment and serious relationship challenges. It was just too easy for him to have as many women as he wanted as the phone calls and texts were always prevalent. As a musician, it was just a normal practice to attract this type of attention.

Only two women, Rheta and now Adria were able to reach into his heart. All of the other women tried repeatedly to get him to seriously love them, but just did not have what it took to get there. This entire awareness caused him to be convicted about his interaction with Mary. And on tonight, after speaking with James, he was even more repentant and had to accept his responsibility for this situation.

It was hard to receive the fact that at this point, he was still dealing with some of those same demons. This is the scenario that could result in him to possibly lose Adria's love and it was costly.

Bryson sighed heavily. He admitted he and Adria were not as connected as they were before. It saddened and even frightened him to think that their relationship might not be able to sustain this turbulence.

Bryson picked up his phone and texted Adria. She quickly replied that she was preparing for bed and would call him in the morning. Bryson prayed and then decided tonight was the night he would seek forgiveness for his actions not just from God, but from Mary and allow his life to be liberated. He called Mary.

She answered stoically, with no emotion in her voice.

"I was wondering if I could come over," he asked, after greeting her.

Mary hesitated and then finally stated, "Sure."

"Okay, I'm leaving now and will see you in a few minutes."

☙

Once Adria arrived home, she showered and prepared herself for bed. She was drained from all the day's activities and thought a cup of herbal tea would help her focus on sleep and slumber.

When she received the text message from Bryson, she was in her study sitting at the desk. She quickly texted him back and stared at her phone afterwards for a while, realizing how much she really missed their late-night talks. Well, she was going to remedy that.

Adria opened her desk drawer and picked a card from the box of blank cards and envelopes; she chose one card and began to write from her heart. In the message, she shared with Bryson her decision to remain with him, no matter the outcome of the DNA test. She shared she was no longer willing to sacrifice the true love she had found with Bryson and knew if they worked together, they would be a formidable force and could get through anything.

After completing the card, she walked into the bedroom and climbed under the bed covers. The herbal tea was relaxing her on the inside, as intended. Adria placed the cup on the nightstand before snuggling into her pillows and comforter, closed her eyes and prepared to drift off to sleep. Before she was finally in the deep sleep stage, the phone text message notification sounded. Adria had forgotten to place the phone on silent and reached over to do so as she checked the message.

The text was from one of her friends Evelyn to whom she once shared an apartment a few years ago. The friend sent a picture and a link regarding a former acquaintance with some devastating news. The news link stated the person was found deceased in a hotel room from an apparent drug overdose.

Adria sat quickly up in her bed and returned the text. Then she pressed the call button in haste. The two cried at the news of someone they spent lots of time with at one point in their lives. At the end of the conversation, Adria re-positioned her pillows behind her as she continued to cry for someone she spent a lot of time with as she learned to live with her newfound freedom.

The friend, Tiffani, was the 'event planner' of the group and ensured their weekly partying was always on point! Adria also knew Tiffani and J had a very close friendship. She frowned as she knew that Tiffani's connection with J allowed her access to many of the perks he offered. Maybe it was being connected with J is what caused her to get addicted to drugs.

Adria felt awful about her former friend's death and was forced to face the hard truths her employment with J probably caused others to become addicts. When Adria worked as his gift-wrapping assistant, she looked the other way as the people who received the gifts were well-off. She wondered how many of them had to sacrifice their quality of life for their pleasures. Adria also wondered how many others suffered greatly from the addictions of which she had no knowledge.

Adria tried to comfort herself from the deep remorse she felt and attempted to relax on her pillows. She became even more saddened as she grieved her former friend's death. She eventually got up from her bed and moved into the living room and sat on the recliner. It was here she began to pray and ask God for forgiveness and asking for him to heal her brokenness. She sobbed as she prayed for Tiffani's soul and for those whose lives she negatively impacted by looking the other way. After a while, her mind and emotions settled enough to enable her to drift off to sleep.

Dr. Paula Y. Obie

Chapter 12
Prayer Changes Things and Prayer Changes People

Bryson arrived at Mary's apartment and knocked. She answered the door shortly.

"Come in," Mary said.

"Thanks," Bryson responded as he took his seat in the chair in the living room area.

Once Mary sat on the couch Bryson began to speak.

"I am not going to keep you, but I came by to say I never meant to hurt or mislead you. I apologize and ask for your forgiveness if I did. You and this child will be a part of my life and my family's life, and we will respect you as their mother. And he or she will already have a big brother named Duane and will grow up as siblings. I just want to know for sure, Mary. I hope you understand why I am so adamant about knowing if this child is mine. Again, I am sorry, and I just want to not live in this cloud of meanness and ugliness anymore. I hope you can accept my apology."

Then Bryson stopped and waited for an answer. He looked over at Mary. Mary had her head turned to the side and remained silent. It seemed like she wanted to say something but could not find the words to verbalize. They sat there like that for a few minutes before Bryson realized It would be best for him to go.

"Anyway, thanks for letting me come by and have my say. I will see myself out."

Bryson then walked out of her apartment and got into his car. He drove home with the music playing softly in the background, his mind reflecting on today's events. Once he was home, he finally settled down and prepared for bed. As he placed his phone on the charger, it illuminated. Mary was calling him.

"Hello," Bryson answered as he walked throughout his home.

"Hey, Bryson...," Mary stated softly, "I thought a lot about what you said when you were here. I appreciate it a lot. I have also said some ugly things to you that I didn't mean, so I hope you can forgive me too. I was just angry and felt rejected." She paused, as if gathering her courage and sighed. "Listen, I decided to have the DNA test done."

There were a few moments of silence. Bryson closed his eyes tightly and silently mouthed the words, "Thank you, God!"

"Can you set up the appointment and just let me know the details. I'll be there," Mary said.

"Sure," Bryson responded, nodding his head. "Thanks, Mary. And again, I will take care of all of the costs."

Adria's Transformation

She said goodnight and hung up. The call was disconnected, and Bryson was feeling even more revitalized.

The following day, the paternity test was scheduled for the current week. The technician took a blood sample from Mary and swabbed Bryson's mouth. The whole thing was painless, simple, and over in a matter of minutes. Then the waiting began. Bryson continued to text Adria daily, but he decided to wait until he had the results in hand to give her the news.

☙

It had been over a week since Adria received the news of Tiffani's death. The services were held on the following Saturday, so she left on a Friday to be there the night before and for the services on the next day.

Adria and Evelyn spent Friday night with the family for a while and learned even more about Tiffani. She was a good girl who was just her own person. She was described as one who would try something first and ask questions later and push herself to the limits –like sky diving or zip lining. Not one story told by a family member blamed anyone for her death—they just seemed to accept the reality she got addicted to "the streets" to something she could not handle.

The celebration of life was to be held at her home church and was filled with her hometown residents and friends to join the family in saying goodbye to Tiffani.

Adria arose early and met Evelyn to attend the viewing before the family arrived. The church was filled with lovely flowers and plants. One flower arrangement, with the letters "TIFF" was magnificently displayed and sat on a pedestal. Adria reached over to read the card and it was from the "Diamonds", which was the name of the group of friends she met when she first left her hometown. Adria and Evelyn sat in the back of the church and listened to the beautiful tributes. The homages delivered focus on Tiffani's vibrant life before she became "controlled by the streets".

On the way back home, Adria thought even more about the turn of events within the past week. Of course, she shared the news of her friend's demise with Bryson, Carla, and her family as well as her plans to attend the service. This entire situation was another sobering moment for Adria to the reality of the consequences of life's choices. It had to remain a constant message in her ear.

Adria and Evelyn parted ways after the burial and promised to talk in a week. Then Adria began her drive back to Rockville. As she motored down the highway, Adria thought of all the changes she had undergone since her return home. Although there were many adjustments, each of them pushed Adria to the person she was created to be, to the person she wanted to be, to live the life she deserved, the one God planned for her.

The drive afforded Adria more than enough time to think about Bryson and their budding love life, or rather the life they were building a few weeks ago. She was a witness of how things could change seemingly overnight. But, unlike Tiffani, she was afforded another chance at life and true happiness. Adria understood that life was not always fair. It had been hard not to jump to unnecessary conclusions over the last few weeks. Each day of waiting for Mary to consent to the paternity test and her just not knowing the truth caused Adria to be more protective of her feelings and leery of her future. And in that, Douglas became her only confidant.

But since she made up her mind to not walk away from her relationship with Bryson no matter what, Adria knew she needed to talk to Bryson about her decision. Tiffani's death had hampered her timing, but she couldn't wait any longer. The realities were illuminated, and the risks stared her in the face. But at this point, her need to fight for the relationship became more important than her need to run away from it.

Adria thought about holding Bryson's hand. This was the moment of truth for her, remembering something so simple. But it caused her to pause and ask herself *why* she did not have the power to just *press* the play button on her life. She couldn't control whether the child was Bryson's, but she could control how she responded. If it were Bryson's child, then, yes, she was going to need lots of love and patience to handle the new reality, but there would be no more punishing innocent children because of grown-up's self-centered, carelessness and foolish decisions.

Adria was also feeling better or rather vindicated, especially after she had her conversation with Francine. She fought the urge to confront Mary directly and tell her that no matter what, she was *not* going to end the relationship with Bryson. Adria was ready to remain loyal to Bryson, and she hoped to God she was not making a fool of herself.

Adria looked up to see the Rockville city limits sign and felt a sense of home and familiarity. Once safely inside of her residence, she contacted her family, Douglas, and Carla to report she had made it home safely. Now, she was ready to relax and talk to Bryson.

☙

Bryson heard the sound of the familiar ringtone for Adria and answered it.

"Hello!" Bryson answered.

"Hi there!" Adria responded.

"Are you home yet?"

"Yes, I am safely in my home and am calling to let you know I am back," Adria stated.

"I am glad you called me," he shared. "Are you tired from driving?"

"I am a little bit tired, but I am okay, though," Adria confessed. "Have you had dinner?"

"No, I have not," Bryson acknowledged.

"Would you like to come over for pizza and wings?" she asked. "I know you don't stay out too late on Saturdays."

"Hmm, pizza and wings sound good," Bryson stated. "I'll be over shortly; I just won't stay too late as you know Sundays are a long day for me."

"Well, text me what kind of pizza and wings you want, and I will place the order," Adria said.

"Text is on the way!" Bryson replied. "See you soon!"

A short while later, Bryson and Adria were settled in her living room, enjoying their favorite pizza and wings. Although this had been an emotional day for Adria, she really wanted to see Bryson.

"Thanks for dinner, Adria," Bryson stated as he leaned back with a full and satisfied stomach. He was seated in her living room chair near the couch.

Adria's Transformation

Adria sat at the corner of her sofa. She wiped her mouth with a napkin after munching on a pizza slice. "You are welcome."

"I was thinking you would have taken a shower and, in the bed, relaxing by now, especially after your drive back," Bryson said.

"I am probably going to be very sleepy in a few minutes," Adria responded smiling. She reached over and retrieved the envelope from underneath a book on the side table. "But I wanted to give you this. I was going to give it to you on tomorrow after church, but I changed my mind." Adria announced.

Bryson reached over and took the envelope with a quick look at Adria. He opened it and retrieved the card within. Adria sat back on the couch and watched him intently as he read the card. Bryson had no immediate reaction until he read the entire contents of the card, twice. In the end, he smiled gently and placed it back into the envelope.

"I made the decision that I'm going to stand by you no matter what. I don't want our relationship to end," Adria said. "I have never loved like this ever before and I am not going to let it go. God gives second and third chances, Bryson. I am not sure which number this is for me, but I am grateful to be here, with you!"

Bryson got up and sat beside his girl on the sofa and gave her a big hug and the two shared the first real kiss in weeks.

"I am so glad to hear it," Bryson stated with a deep sigh of relief. "I just don't know how I would have been able to get through all of this without you beside me." He then gave her another big hug and they shared a deeper, longer, more passionate kiss.

Dr. Paula Y. Obie

Chapter 13
In Due Season

Bryson instructed the lab to send his test results to the church office via certified mail. Promptly on the seventh working day the package was delivered by the post office. Bryson opened the document and the test confirmed he was *not* the father of Mary's unborn child. He turned his chair around so that he peered out his office window with the results in his hands.

"Man, oh man, this was a close one," he confessed with relief. He closed his eyes and began to thank God for once again protecting him from himself. He felt like he had been given another chance, just as Adria had said. Bryson struggled with many habits that did not immediately vanish after his re-dedication to the Lord. He still needed spiritual, emotional growth and maturity to help him along the way, but at least now he could move forward without worrying about the mistakes of his past.

Bryson opened his eyes and relaxed completely in his chair as he slightly rocked left to right. He heard the knock on the office door and after giving the person permission to enter, he found himself looking into the eyes of his Bishop.

Bryson smiled slightly and stated five words, "God is a good God," and gave him the results. Bishop looked them over and with a big smile on his face, said, "Yes, He is son. Yes, He is!" Bishop walked out of Bryson's office whistling and thanking God for His tender mercies. "God is an awesome God," he sang, "He is an awesome God and greatly to be praised."

Bryson returned his thoughts to Adria. He thought of how she had handled their initial crisis as a couple. He saw how she became increasingly distant, and their communication grew strained. Nor did she smile much, but then neither of them had anything really to smile about.

When he went to visit her unannounced and they went for a walk, it was the first time he had held her hand in a while, but it felt awkward and there was a lot of silence.

Then a miracle happened, and she let him know she would stick by him. He was so thrilled by her announcement that all he could think to do was start dancing right there in the living room. But he remained reserved and welcomed the wonderful hugs and kisses of their reconnection.

He leaned back in his chair and allowed himself to exhale, incredibly grateful and cognizant that this situation could have turned out so differently for him.

Bryson placed the paperwork back in the large envelope and prepared to share the news with Adria.

Bishop called Bryson's extension and asked him to stop by his office before leaving the church on today. Bryson readied himself for a father-son discussion his pastor always offered during crucial times.

Adria's Transformation

Bryson also felt it was an optimal moment for him to share with Bishop the deep corridors of his heart—his dreams, desires, goals, and immediate plans. He thought of the ring he purchased for Adria several weeks ago and how it still sat on his nightstand.

Plans needed to be made quickly so he could deliver the results to Adria and his family. For now, first things first: Bryson needed to prepare for the meeting with the Bishop.

☙

It was 3:00 p.m. on Saturday and Adria's cell phone rang. It was Bryson, who had completed all his rehearsals and now had the remainder of the afternoon free. He asked Adria to meet him at their favorite ice cream shop.

Once Bryson and Adria were seated at the table and eating their ice cream, he handed her a white envelope.

"What's this?" Adria asked casually.

"Just look at it."

Adria placed the spoon in her ice cream cup of rainbow sherbet and sat it on the table. Then she removed the paperwork from the envelope. It was the results of a DNA test. Adria's eyes grew wide as she read that Bryson was not the father. She placed her hand over her mouth. Adria was beyond thrilled. She felt like she could actually hear her life being taken off *pause*.

"When did this happen?" she asked, shocked.

Bryson shared James' story of how he and Mary had been together for months and how Mary consented to have the prenatal test. Bryson also reported that James had the DNA test taken, which proved he was the father of Mary's baby. James had called Bryson the previous evening to give him the news.

"We can finally get out of this holding pattern and start living our lives again," Adria declared.

"True!" Bryson stated.

"I know this is none of my business," Adria stated, "But I feel really badly for James and hope this all works out for him. Does he know what he is getting himself into?"

"Not sure," Bryson confessed, as he reached over and held both of Adria's hands. "But he is willing to try."

He took a deep breath and exhaled.

"Whew! These last few weeks have been really long. But I am glad to be in this place, with you!" Bryson added with a smile.

Adria smiled back. She continued to review the results and then thought about Francine, wondering if she was aware of James and Mary's relationship. After a moment, though, she refused to think long about Mary or Francine. Her full attention was on Bryson and their future.

Chapter 14
Let's Do This Right

Bryson and Adria wanted to celebrate this night with their friends and their closest four couples agreed to meet for dinner. Everyone was happy to be together and enjoying a good meal. It was a fun time and provided the setting and company suitable for this type of occasion. Bryson and Adria shared a happiness tonight that had been missing in their relationship for weeks. The group left the restaurant laughing, joking and in a terrific mood.

Later, Adria and Bryson took their usual after dinner walk. For a while they strolled in silence. Words were not necessary as they ambled hand-in-hand down a familiar path, taking a few minutes every now and then to glance at each other and smile.

Bryson led Adria to the nearest bench and motioned for her to be seated. He bowed and pointed to the seat as if they were in the Victorian age. Adria curtsied dramatically and held her clothes as if she wore a long petticoat dress and then sat down and adjusted her 'imaginary' gown.

The humorous atmosphere from the dinner table had not subsided. The two were still giddy from the reality of the test results and the impact of being in a happy group setting.

Bryson sat down beside Adria. He looked at her and then started to speak.

"Adria, you are so special to me. In fact, you are just an extra special woman and I want you to know how much I've appreciated your support these past few weeks. I know you wanted to just go off and tell me to get lost at times, but you never did."

Adria remained silent and bit down on her lower lip as he talked.

"I don't know anyone else who would have treated me so kindly. I didn't know what you were going to do, and things were moving very slowly," Bryson continued. "But you have this..." He looked towards the sky, with his eyes slowly darting left and right as if listening to God before stating, "...quiet peace, and it runs deep. I guess your life experiences taught you not to panic over every little thing ... I don't know."

Adria continued to remain silent, but a smile was creeping on her lips and inwardly declared, "If only you knew ..."

"I just want to say thank you so much for believing in me and in us. You are remarkable, smart, beautiful, anointed and I am not sure why you love me, but I am glad you do."

Adria laughed out loud but still did not speak. An inner voice told her to 'be still.'

"I think the love we have is the kind of love that works. If it lasted through this fiasco and survived, it can last through anything. So, do you feel we could grow old together?" Bryson inquired.

Adria's Transformation

"I believe you and I could do that," Adria answered as she glanced at Bryson's face.

"We haven't had a fight yet though and can't get married before it happens. I certainly don't want that type of surprise," Bryson teased.

"Yes, I do have a temper, but only when I am pushed to a certain point. I try hard to be fair but when I am really angry, I don't care about what other people think at all," Adria explained. "Are you shocked?"

"Not really. I'm glad we are talking about it. I was thinking I would see more anger from you with the situation with Mary," Bryson confessed. "Did you hold it all inside?"

"I guess," Adria replied. She did not feel it was the optimal time to discuss her therapy sessions and would save this topic for a later date.

"I like the open communication between us. I am not accustomed to having such an honest approach in life," Bryson said. Then he stood up and positioned himself on one knee in front of Adria. "Why should we waste time? I told you in the beginning of our relationship, I wanted to do this thing right and have God's blessing in every area of my life," He continued. "Since you and I have been together, I have grown, really grown, in so many ways. Your love has changed me into the man I knew I could be and *was already* deep down on the inside. In these past few weeks, though, I was troubled by the thought of losing you forever and it stayed on my mind, night, and day. If I had to, I was willing to resign from my job at GFCC and just work diligently on us, no matter what! That's when I knew I had the right one, the right woman, the help mate I deserved, and I needed to convince you to stay with me."

Then he reached into his jacket pocket and brought out a heart-shaped ring enclosed with baguettes diamonds. Adria immediately realized what was happening, but she felt like she was in a dream. Bryson then dropped to one knee, reached for her hand, and placed the ring on her finger.

"So, will you marry me?" Bryson asked.

Adria heard the question with her ears first, and then her heart. She looked initially at the exquisite ring on her finger and then at Bryson. Then she responded happily, "Yes, yes, yes, yes, yes, yes, yes, yes!"

Adria threw her arms around Bryson's neck, and they hugged each other tightly. They pulled away after a moment, and looked deeply into each other's eyes, before sealing this moment with a kiss. When the kiss ended, they stood up and continued their walk. However, every few steps, Adria stopped walking and looked at her left hand.

"Bryson, this ring is gorgeous. When did you get it?" Adria gushed.

"Let's just say I've had it for a little while," he said.

Adria couldn't stop smiling.

"This is the type of feeling I hoped I would have when I became engaged. I am so excited," Adria shared.

Bryson smiled but remained silent as they walked towards the car. But about halfway through their stroll, Bryson took her hand and pulled her to him and broke out into a dance. Adria joined him, as they did a 'waltz' dance together. They did not care who saw them. This was their happy moment and their happy dance.

A couple of other walkers strolled past them and giggled as if they understood Bryson and Adria were in a very special moment.

Adria's Transformation

As soon as Bryson returned Adria to her residence, she rushed into the house to dial her parents' home phone to share the news.

"Hi Mama!" Adria stated after Mama Darden answered the phone. "Guess what? Bryson asked me to marry him tonight," Adria blurted out excitedly.

"He what?" her mom asked with her voice sounding surprised. "Did you say 'Yes'?"

"Yes, I did." Adria smiled as she spoke, singing the word 'did.'

"John, pick up the phone, your daughter has something to tell you," Mrs. Darden yelled.

Adria heard the landline extension being picked up by her daddy. "Hey honey bun, what's going on?" He asked. She also heard the other phone being placed on its base and Adria envisioned Mama Darden walking into the same room as her husband so they all could talk at the same time.

"Put her on the speaker," Mama Darden directed. Once he did, Adria exclaimed, "Daddy, Bryson Kenton asked me to marry him, and I said yes!"

"You did?" Papa Darden replied. "I really like him; I think the two of you will do fine together. As a matter of fact, he asked me and your Mom for your hand in marriage and we were waiting for him to pop the question."

"When did he ask you that?" Adria asked shocked.

"Never mind when. He is a little bit old fashioned, and you should be proud he cared enough about your parents to get our permission first," Papa Darden remarked.

"Daddy, I am thirty-three years old, what were you going to say?" Adria laughed.

"I have been waiting for you to get married for the longest. I certainly was not going to say 'No'. I thought I was going to have to spend your wedding money on something else," Papa Darden teased.

"What wedding money?" Adria inquired, again shocked at what her Poppie was telling her.

"We have been saving up money for your wedding since the day you were born," Mama Darden confessed. "It's been sitting there waiting for you and I just prayed it would happen while your Dad and I were still alive and able to enjoy the ceremony and could also be in the pictures!"

"Wow! I had no idea." Adria responded gently as this was the very first time anyone had even mentioned having this type of financial preparation.

"When are you going to tell your brothers?" Mama Darden asked.

"I will call them next and share the news," Adria stated cheerfully.

"You are going to have very little problems with all of them except one, who seems to have a major issue with Mr. Bryson Kenton," Mama Darden reported. "I am not sure what happened between them two, but it is not resolved after all of these years."

"Wonderful," Adria muttered with a disgusted sound in her voice.

"Now, the real question is, are you ready to tell your sister?" Papa Darden asked.

Adria sighed. "Yes, I am ..."

"Honey bun, you and your sister are going to have to find a way to get along. You have got to stop this feud. We all need to sit down and straighten all of this out as soon as possible. It's been going on way too long," Papa Darden declared.

"She told us about your latest encounter," Mama Darden added. "What in the world was going on with you that you would go to her house and start an argument?"

"There was no argument, Mama, I just told her my truth," Adria responded gently. "Mary and Francine were playing games and I needed to let her know I was no longer willing to overlook it!"

Mama Darden sighed heavily before continuing.

"We all know Mary has always had her issues. She and Francine have been friends for a long time. Francine has involved herself in many areas of Mary's life and some things have gone too far," Mama Darden said. "Your Dad and I talked to Francine, so now we all need to get together and sort this all out. Especially now!"

"We are family and we gotta work this out somehow," Papa Darden added.

With a sigh, Adria acknowledged, "You are right Poppie, you are right".

"Well," Mrs. Darden stated out loud in a cheerful voice, "I guess we need to start getting ready for a wedding."

☙

Bryson drove out to the home place. He planned to deliver a package to his father and thought it was a perfect segue to telling them the good news. He drove up to his usual spot, rang the doorbell and let himself in through the side door.

"Hey Mom! Hey Pop!" Bryson announced cheerfully.

He found his parents in the family room sitting in their favorite chairs and watching television.

"Hey son! How are you doing?" his mother exclaimed.

"I am good, Mom," Bryson stated. "Pop, I left your fishing pole on the back porch." He walked over and gave his mom a kiss on the cheek.

"Thank you!" Mr. Kenton stated. "Have a seat, Son."

"I have a few minutes," Bryson remarked and made himself comfortable on the couch.

The three of them chatted for a while before Bryson was ready to share the news.

"Guess what I did earlier this evening?" Bryson asked. His parents looked at him with anticipation. "I asked Adria to marry me, and she said 'Yes'," Bryson reported, beaming from ear to ear.

"You what?" Mrs. Kenton exclaimed cheerfully. She grinned while Mr. Kenton stood up and moved in the direction of his son. They hugged.

Mrs. Kenton stood patiently and waited for her turn to hug her son. After the first hug she stood back and laughed aloud while clapping her hands. Then she hugged him a second time before returning to her recliner.

"Well, congratulations, son," Mr. Kenton grinned as he patted his son on the back. "Mama, can you believe it? The two of them are going to get married. We watched her when she was a child and now, she's back and going to be our daughter-in-law!"

Mrs. Kenton didn't hear him because she was already calling the rest of the family members and telling them the good news. "Here, talk to your sister," she said, handing the phone to Bryson. As he talked to Tara, Mr. Kenton grabbed his cell phone and called his brother. It was total chaos in the Kenton family when the news finally circled.

ଔ

On the next day Adria and Francine agreed to meet at Papa and Mama Darden's house for a heart-to-heart discussion after their church services ended. The four of them were seated around the dining room table admiring the beautiful heart-shaped pink diamond baguette engagement ring on Adria's left ring finger.

"Wow, this ring is expensive," Mama Darden remarked. "He sure has excellent taste."

Papa Darden shot an eye at Mama Darden to just let the sisters talk as they previously agreed. He had already beforehand spoken to each of his daughters individually and given them the charge to fix this problem as soon as possible! After a moment of silence, they began talking.

"Why did you come over to my house and pick a fight with me?" Francine asked curtly.

"I didn't come over to your house to pick a fight with you, Francine," Adria confirmed, "I came over to have a conversation and own my truths. I mean, I'm your sister, but you take Mary's side on everything. Why are you so angry with me?"

Francine did not answer her immediately. Adria could see her eyes mist over, then one tear rolled down her cheek.

"You left me here and I didn't know what to do... nobody was here for me ...you didn't even come back and get me. You didn't care about me anymore!" she stated, angrily.

"That's not true—" Adria insisted, but Francine didn't seem to hear her and kept talking.

"You left me, abandoned me and then you came back and all of a sudden you are getting all of this attention and with Bryson Kenton, of all people," Francine admitted with an angry voice. "The man that everybody wanted!" Francine then rolled her eyes for emphasis at the last statement before continuing. "He messed over Rheta and messed over Mary." Her voice trailed off before she quietly added. "And...maybe I was still upset that he never acknowledged what I felt for him when I was younger...

Adria's eyebrows shot up. She wondered if Bryson knew.

"I didn't know that," she said quietly.

Francine shrugged her shoulders, but she didn't look at her sister, only turned her face away from her.

"It's in the past. It doesn't matter."

Adria felt like it did, and though she was glad that Francine had shared her truth, she now needed to speak hers.

"Well, I did not come back home for Bryson Kenton," Adria stated, "I came back because I could not live another moment away from my family. I wanted to reconnect with everybody; and I knew you and I were not in a good place, and I wanted to try and fix that, but I can't fix everything overnight, I am not God."

Adria waited but Francine remained silent. Papa Darden jumped into the conversation.

"Francine and Adria, are you willing to let this go and you two start forgiving each other?" Papa Darden

Adria's Transformation

asked. "We cannot continue to live this way. I know there are a lot of folks who have bad feelings for their family members, but it doesn't make it right and this family has to do better. We need to stop pretending when it hurts. Nobody is perfect."

"I guess so," Francine stated quietly. There was a moment of silence and then Adria also responded, "Yes."

Adria walked over to her sister, sat beside of her, and squeezed her hard. Francine began crying loudly, her sobs filling the room. Adria hugged her and they held onto each other, crying for the times they lost, and for the pain, tears, and misunderstandings.

Eventually Papa Darden and Mama Darden left the dining room to give their daughters the space they needed to work through this crisis.

"Well, let's start over today and try to treat each other right," Adria requested. "I love you, Francine."

"I love you too, Adria."

And even in that, Adria understood the conversation had only just begun.

"Francine, I am thirty-three years old, and I never thought I'd find somebody like Bryson. I consider it a gift from God, I really do," Adria said as she wiped away her tears. "I didn't even know how to love, much less love anyone like this. Gerrard used to tell me when I found someone to love I would fall really, really hard, and I have, and I don't regret it. And to be honest, these last few weeks, I had Bryson under a high-powered microscope while he was dealing with this situation with Mary." Adria sighed. "You find out a lot about somebody when they are under that type of pressure."

"I told you he was a womanizer," Francine stated cynically, as she wiped up her face.

Adria glared at her sister before responding. "Your friend Mary really needs to get some help. Don't point the finger entirely at him."

"Well, he must have slept with her at least once, or else she would have not have even brought it up," Francine argued on Mary's behalf.

"But she was having a secret relationship with James. Did you know that? And it turned out he is the father of her child," Adria added.

Francine glared at her. She didn't seem surprised at the news, maybe a little resigned. "I knew she was hanging out with someone, but I didn't know who he was, and I didn't know they were sleeping together."

"It's none of my business, but James seems to really love her," Adria stated. "So, can we let this go now? As you said, it's all in the past. It doesn't matter anymore."

"Are you absolutely sure he won't do that to you?" Francine asked.

Adria didn't have to think about her response.

"Yes. Yes, I am."

Francine studied her face and finally nodded.

"Good," Adria said. "Now, are you going to give me your blessing and be my matron of honor?"

"I guess so, "Francine stated and eventually smiled. She gave her sister another big hug. "I don't trust this guy one hundred percent yet...but I am willing to give him a chance for your sake."

Adria smiled. That was the most she could ask for right now, and she would take it.

"Thank you."

Adria and Francine finished speaking and joined Mama Darden in the kitchen, to complete the meal she started

Adria's Transformation

earlier. Eventually, Adria's brothers, Andrew, Darius, and Isaac, joined them. They came into the house with a lot of loud commotion and excitement.

"Hi Pop!" said Andrew. "Thank God, we are finally gonna marry this one off!" He then broke into a holy dance. The rest of the brothers joined in with the dancing, shouting, and clapping their hands. The laughter broke out in a chorus when Adria walked out of the kitchen with her hands on her hips and a 'fake' angry look on her face.

"I am not even thinking about ya'll," she said with a dramatic neck action and the pointer finger waving back and forth. Then she walked back over to the dining room table and sat in one of the chairs as they made their way into the area.

The sons headed to the kitchen to say hello to Mama Darden and to see what she was cooking. Once they said their hello's and were satisfied with the menu, they joined Adria.

The family meal was finally ready to be served. Once everyone was seated at the table and Papa Darden said the grace, dinner commenced and discussions about Adria's engagement announcement began.

"So, exactly how long have you two been dating, anyway?" asked Isaac.

"We started dating at the end of spring. Our official first date was April 6th."

"So why are you in such a hurry, you don't even know this guy," continued Darius. "And don't tell me, 'We grew up together,' because it was a long time ago."

"It's no hurry, we're just ready," Adria explained. "Both of our lives have been enriched since we started dating."

"We have to admit he has an incredible gift. Everyone brags about his musical ability," says Andrew.

"Yes, he is talented, but is he going to take care of my sister?" barked Darius.

"Bryson can afford her," says Mama Darden. "Just look at this engagement ring?"

"In addition to his financial status," Adria stated, "he really is a good guy."

"Well, what I want to know is if he is going to have any money left over after his child support payments?" asked Darius. "Is he making that much money as a full-time Ministers of Music?"

"And how many kids does he have?" asked Isaac.

"I heard he has a lot of them. I mean when you have a history of sleeping with so many women, what else can you expect?" asked Darius.

Thankfully, Francine remained quiet during this exchange. Still, Adria didn't like how her brothers were ganging up on Bryson. She squinted her eyes before responding.

"Wait a minute! Are we really having this conversation? What man doesn't have a reputation?" Adria retorted. "Lord knows, I have had to defend your characters since you all started dating." She continued emphatically. "And.... how many times have you all been accused of having a baby by every girl you have been with?" Adria then looked directly at Darius, and raised her hand, "What is going on with you and Bryson? Why are you so angry with him?"

"It's a long story," Darius admitted.

"We got time," says Mama Darden. Papa Darden who stood to go get another beverage quickly returned to sit in the dining chair to hear the story.

Adria's Transformation

Darius sighed and described multiple childhood and teenage experiences that caused them to be archrivals. At one point, they had even competed for the same girl, which caused bad blood between them.

"So let me get this straight, you were rivals on the court, rivals in the field, rivals in the church district organization and rivals...over women?" Adria repeated.

"When are you going to get over it?" Mama Kenton asked. "You both are grown men now."

"Bryson and I love each other, and the love is real and strong. You all just need to accept that." Adria paused for a second. "This situation with Mary brought us closer, and even if the child had been his, I still would have chosen him. I would have had to work harder to stay positive, but I would still love him. I am sure of it," she added. "So, can I please have your support? Will you please get to know Bryson? I promise you this much: if you find something that is going to take me out like Gerrard, then I will listen because I am not getting married to live in hell or in that kind of farce or misery." Adria affirmed.

The room became silent as everyone reflected on Gerrard and his life. Eventually, it was Darius who spoke. "I will kill him if he does not do right by you, and I am not playing. I won't have time to ask a whole bunch of questions either."

"Calm down!" commanded Mama Darden as she looked first at her son and then back at Adria. "Bryson's a good guy. Although he had a little bit of a reputation with the women, I think he was just looking for the right woman. And my daughter is the right woman. Adria made the right decision for her, so leave this bad blood at the table and let's start getting ready for a wedding."

Dr. Paula Y. Obie

Chapter 15
The Engagement Party

The Darden's and Kenton's met and planned the engagement party for Adria and Bryson, discussing everything that needed to be done. At 5:30 p.m. Adria, Bryson and Duane arrived at the restaurant where they were holding the party. Then at 6:00 p.m., the rest of the family members walked through the doors and into the private party room. Adria, Bryson, and Duane were seated at the largest table along with the parents. Papa Darden welcomed everyone and stated the reason for their gathering. Adria smiled at her father and had always admired his charming personality and great sense of humor.

"We want to thank you all for coming to this official engagement party for Adria and Bryson. Lord knows, I have prayed long and hard for this night and to think that in just a few months, these two kids will be husband and wife." Papa Darden smiled at Adria and Bryson. "Bryson who would have thought all of those times we were together in church you would become a part of our family and the father of my future grandchildren. The Lord truly works in mysterious ways!"

The room erupted with laughter. Papa Darden waited until it died down before continuing. "We are so thankful you all are here. Mrs. Darden and I are pleased to have us all soon be officially joined together. We'll have the grace by Mr. Kenton and then we'll be ready to eat."

Mr. Kenton arose from his chair. "Yes, we too, are very excited to be here tonight to get to know the Darden's even more and are delighted to have Adria as a part of our family. No, we never dreamed this would happen, but we are thankful to God it has. May we bow our heads."

After the grace, Francine stood and introduced herself and to announce that the elderly and the family members who desired, would be served by the two waiters in the back. Everyone else was to be led to the buffet. Adria and Bryson allowed the others to go through the buffet first and talked with several family members who walked over to them.

When everyone had gotten their food and were eating, Papa Darden let them know it was time for the family to hear from Adria and Bryson. Bryson signaled for Adria to talk first and she stood appropriately and began to speak.

"Bryson is one of the nicest men I have ever met in my life. If I had created my ideal profile of the boyfriend, fiancé and soon to be husband, it would be Bryson and I am grateful." Adria took a deep breath before continuing. She looked at Bryson lovingly. "Gerrard used to warn me that when I finally fell in love for real, I would fall really, really hard. Well, he was right and here we are just a few months and a lot of details away from the big date. Thank you all for coming tonight and I look forward to our future gatherings and our being together as a family from now on."

At the conclusion of her speech, she sat and looked at Bryson signaling she was finished, and it was his turn. Bryson stood at the end of the applause and cleared his throat.

"What can I say? When Adria came to GFCC and walked up to me to say hello, I immediately knew who she was. I thought about how long it had been since I had seen her and how close our families used to be. It was *not* love at first sight, but it was shortly thereafter. Admitting I was in love with her was easier once I told myself she was my answered prayer and that I deserved her. I am thankful to have you all as my new family and I look forward to great family times together."

Bryson reached down and signaled for Adria to stand. "Isn't she beautiful and in a few months, she will be mine! Thank you, Jesus!"

The room erupted into laughter and applause at Bryson's boldness. Adria started laughing and sweetly placed her hand on the small of his back. The two of them exchanged a loving look. Then Adria returned to her seat.

Bryson started singing a popular praise and worship song. The room joined in. The moment was special and heartfelt, with a beautiful ending to signify the uniting of two God-fearing families. It topped off a perfect evening.

The dinner ended and Papa Darden made his way to the register to pay the bill. Within a matter of minutes, he was smiling as he walked towards his family with his toothpick sticking out of the side of his mouth. Everyone gave their goodbye hugs and left the restaurant and walked into the parking lot.

Adria and Bryson exited the engagement party holding hands as they walked to the car. It was agreed Duane would spend some time with Mr. and Mrs. Kenton for the remainder of the evening. Bryson would retrieve his son on the following day. They considered it their special time together, as they did not get to see him as often as they desired anymore.

Bryson opened the passenger door and Adria sat in the seat. They drove close to his mother and father's vehicle and signaled for his mom to lower the window.

"You two are the best and I love you," Bryson stated. "Love you little man, be sweet!"

"Bye Daddy," responded Duane as he excitedly waved at Bryson from his booster seat waiting for his grandparents to exit the parking lot.

Bryson then drove over to where the Darden's were standing to give Adria a chance to also have words. Papa and Mama Darden walked over to the car.

"Thank you, so much. I love you!" Adria stated.

"Love you too honey bun. Listen, I'd give you a couple of thousand dollars or so to elope. Just think about it." Papa Darden had a serious look on his face and then at the end of the sentence he grinned broadly. Mama Darden stared momentarily at her husband, but she was not smiling. Bryson and Adria laughed as they drove away.

"What do you think about the eloping idea?" Bryson probed.

Adria smiled at the question. "Oh, I don't know, maybe we should take him up on it. But then we would not have the wonderful pictures, videos and all the other fun stuff. At first, I didn't care about it so much, but now I have gotten really excited about it."

Bryson laughed. "Just think in a few months, we'll be making our own history. As a matter of fact, we are making it now. Did you see the look on our parents' faces? I think they are proud of both of us."

"Yes, they are. And I can't wait," Adria acknowledged, then added, "We will need to start the couples counseling next week with Bishop and First Lady."

"I hear it was quite an intense six-week process. I think we are the only ones in this class this time," Bryson said.

Adria looked into Bryson's face before continuing. "I saw the email the first would be a group session and the others would be one-on-one. Especially if it is the first marriage."

"Well, we will sure find out as our sessions start next Tuesday," Bryson added and glanced at Adria as he continued their drive.

Adria nodded her head slowly and said, "Yes, we will."

☙

At the conclusion of the first marriage counseling session, Bryson and Adria were left with homework and a lot of deep thinking. Adria had a gnawing feeling in her gut at one point, signaling she would need to work diligently to push past her emotions. Bishop had talked about ensuring both parties knew the important facets of each other's lives so they would not be surprised or left defenseless. He said, "Don't allow someone, either your friends or your families or your enemies—and you do have them—to tell your fiancé something you should have shared as it could signal you already have trust issues to work through."

Adria immediately thought about one conversation she had withheld from Bryson that could make a difference in their trust levels. As she knew it was in her past, but if it were to surface, it would be one of those very uncomfortable truths that would cause her problems. Adria prayed God would give her the words and the optimal time for sharing her story with Bryson.

"Whew, what a crazy week I've had!" Bryson remarked as he sighed heavily, as they sat down to have a quiet dinner at a neighborhood restaurant. "It seemed everything had a completion date within the past five days! Bishop gave me a list of requests he wanted that was a mile long. The musicians were having all kinds of issues. Everyone was driving me crazy. I could not wait for the weekend!"

Adria was quite aware Bryson was unusually agitated. He had been in this space for the past couple of weeks. She assumed it was the combination of pressures at work, final wedding music preparation, and the marriage counseling sessions.

The wedding was going to be absolutely fabulous, and she was grateful to an awesomely talented and creative wedding planner with a gracious mother and father who offered unwavering support. But even Adria was not in her usual festive mood. She was starting to have problems resting during the night as her mind was constantly checking and re-checking items on the lists and other preparation activities. Still, she was trying to be supportive of Bryson and take care of herself as well.

Adria's Transformation

Her biggest stressor, though, was the fact that Adria had not found the words yet to reveal to Bryson some important details of her life during the decade she was away. It was weighing heavily on her mind. She knew she needed to talk to him and had been practicing what she would say. But to date, she had not yet found the optimal moment to speak with him regarding a vital part of her life journey.

"The weekend *is* here and it's the weekend you have *off!*" Adria responded. "Is there any way you can wind down a little bit?"

"I am going to try and this dinner with you is a start, sweetie!" Bryson stated curtly.

Adria saw Bryson's phone illuminated repeatedly indicating there was an incoming call. He would glance at the phone, but the new rule was he would not answer it during dinner unless it was an emergency or a call from a person on the high priority list, like his parents, Rheta, or Bishop.

Bryson reached over to eat one of his calamari rings. He grimaced and was visibly frustrated. He dunked it into the garlic butter sauce combination before stuffing it in his mouth.

"You okay, darling?" Adria reached over and touched his hand.

Bryson leaned back in the chair and slowly chewed.

"Why do you ask?" Bryson responded.

"Just a gut feeling...," Adria offered. "I mean, you seem agitated."

"Yes, it was a tough week, as I stated before. I have a lot of things going on, and, if you don't mind, I would rather not talk about it now. I am here with you, and this was the most relaxed I have been all week." Bryson responded. He then placed down his fork and picked up his tea. After returning the glass to the table, he stated joyfully, "It's sixty days and counting!"

"I know. I have begun to not sleep well as I check things off my preparation lists all through the night." Adria added. "I'm really exhausted these days!"

"Isn't it the wedding planner's job to check things off the list?" Bryson inquired as he continued eating his appetizer. "

"Yes, but you know how it is. It's hard to not help out a bit," Adria stated.

"Well, if I were you, I'd let her do her job so you can focus on being the gorgeous bride I know you are going to be because you are going to have to keep up with your *extremely* handsome groom as I know I am going to be looking good!" Bryson dramatically spoke the words in an arrogantly/playful manner. He then returned his attention to his food before asking, "By the way, what's left to do?"

"Just the normal task list two months before the big wedding day," Adria insisted. "Mama has really come alive during the wedding planning. I have not seen her so positive about anything I've been involved in. Don't get me wrong, as she can always find something to whine about, but she has changed so much."

The waiter brought over their entrees and they both started eating. There was an unusual silence between Adria and Bryson. Adria was searching for words as she tried to focus her attention on her food.

"Well at least we completed the couples counseling this week," Adria stated aloud. "It was a really thorough class."

Adria's Transformation

Bryson remained silent as he glanced over at his phone that illuminated repeatedly. He then finally spoke. "And very intense."

Adria was no longer easily distracted by Bryson's phone notifications. She had grown to embrace the responsibilities and level of accountability that are a part of Bryson's calling. Since the scenario with Mary, she had developed a new level of trust. She also accepted the fact Bryson's lifestyle required him to stay in contact with key folks.

Adria had a better understanding regarding family interactions as her own family had also grown closer since she returned to her hometown. As her business tasks at times caused her to work long hours, Bryson was also forced to embrace her responsibilities. They were both busy with spiritual assignments, business tasks and families who needed their attention. In the very near future, they would have to learn to prioritize their marriage into these existing routines.

However, tonight, during her meal, she placed her phone on silent and refused to take it out of her purse while she was enjoying her time with Bryson.

Her heart told her the incoming calls tonight may *not* be church related. Bryson would glance at the phone but refused to answer it. He looked up at Adria and their eyes met. He then looked past her to signal the waiter to fill his beverage glass.

Truthfully, Adria was also distracted and contributed to the atmosphere at their table. She was replaying the words of Bishop and First Lady from the sessions. At the final class they reemphasized the need to share certain truths with your fiancé before, rather than after the marriage. Adria was struggling with the words to discuss a very important fact concerning her past with Bryson.

This was the time when she needed to use her voice. Trying to find her voice was one of the biggest issues she faced in life, and now, that she was going to be married soon, using her voice as a wife was even more vital to her quality of life.

She continued to play with her food as she pondered what to do. For now, she would just focus on Bryson and his mood.

"Sweetie, are you sure everything is okay? You seem unusually distracted tonight!" Adria asked again.

Bryson's facial expression confirmed he did not want to have this discussion at this time.

"I *really* don't want to talk about it while we are eating," Bryson stated.

"You'd rather wait until later?" Adria questioned. "It's your choice, but it's okay with me if you want to take the time to talk now!"

Bryson stopped eating and placed down his fork and knife. "So, you are going to make me talk about it?" Bryson questioned with an edge.

"No, not make you ... just encourage you!" Adria stated as she ate her seafood salad.

"Well ... it feels like you are pressuring me, and I don't want to be pressured right now!" Bryson stated rather sternly.

"I don't want you to feel pressured, darling, just supported. Maybe I can help!" Adria continued. She was still searching for her voice... for her balance on the tightrope she was determined to walk.

CB

Adria's Transformation

Bryson looked at his bride to be, who chose tonight to be extremely assertive and persistent. He had to give her one thing: she was beginning to zero in on his moods. Her radar along with the spirit of discernment was on point. There were major things bothering him and sure, he probably needed to talk to her but did not want to spoil his dinner.

Bryson smiled briefly and responded with a wink and "I love you!"

This reply was enough to alter the mood as Adria echoed his comment with, "I love you too!"

For the rest of the evening, they focused more attention on themselves and their upcoming wedding plans. They discussed in more detail the wedding music and other creative topics. At the conclusion of their meal, the environment was less stressful. However, both remained unusually quiet, indicating their individual levels of distractions and fatigue.

They walked hand-in-hand to the car and chuckled sporadically as they traveled home.

Bryson glanced at his clock to see it was still an early evening, and he was not sure where he wanted to go next. "Are you in the mood for a drive?"

"Sure," Adria quickly responded, then teased, "My boyfriend is not scheduled to be home for another couple of hours, so I am good."

"I'll have you safely home before he gets there, I promise," Bryson returned. He then exited the car onto the freeway and turned on the cruise control. Afterwards, he reached for Adria's hand.

The gospel radio station played one of his favorite songs. Bryson silently sung along with the lyrics and reminded himself he had done all he could at this point.

It was time for him to be prepared to take this situation to another level.

"Adria, I am having a few problems with Rheta," Bryson shared after they had cruised for several miles.

"What kind of problems?" Adria asked with a frown.

"I have not been able to find her at times. She'll tell me to meet her so I can pick up Duane and then call and cancel at the last minute. Then she'll call back and ask for money. I haven't seen my son in a few weeks, and I am starting to get irritated with her," Bryson reported. "We have an agreement and I want him in my life."

"Do you think it's because of our upcoming wedding plans?" Adria asked.

"Could be or she's just not in a good place," Bryson suggested. "She's really been acting very strange and has been unreliable. She came into the office to ask for money, and I asked her where Duane was and she said, 'With a friend'. I asked when I could pick him up to spend some time with him. Rheta made a smart remark and didn't give me an answer," Bryson added. "I figured she was just showing out because of us, and I have been trying to be patient with her, but my patience is growing thin."

"Have you been by her place?" Adria asked.

"Yes, but she's never there. I am wondering if she is even still living there or what is going on. Rheta knows how much I love Duane and could be just using him *again* to cause me problems. She's done it before."

"What are you going to do?" Adria asked softly stroking his arm.

"I am going to have to find a way to connect with her. She called tonight while we were eating and when you went to the bathroom, I checked my voice mail. In the message she stated she and Duane were at a friend's house, and she would call me tomorrow," Bryson reported. "That's been her standard message, but it's several days before she calls."

☙

Adria listened to Bryson's voice and wondered how she could intervene or assist. She thought about suggesting hiring a private investigator, but the timing might not be the best with all the wedding expenses.

"Has she allowed Duane to be fitted for his tux?" Adria further inquired.

"No, that's what started all of this. I wanted him to get fitted and she would never make the appointment. It was always an excuse."

"Hmm," Adria sighed audibly. "It does sound strange."

"Rheta is supposed to call me in the morning."

Adria now understood Bryson's intense mood and how this problem with Duane affected them. Duane was Bryson's heart string and if Rheta was acting carelessly, then Duane could be in jeopardy. It was just another reminder of what Adria's life was going to be like once she was married to Bryson.

Bryson eased the car down Highway 75, listening to the music as they drove to their destination. Bryson exited right onto the street to lead him to the parking lot of the Carrington-Tate Mall. He pulled the car in front of the ice cream shop and parked.

"Do you want some ice cream?" Bryson asked her. It had only been a few minutes since they left the restaurant and Adria had not had dessert.

"Sure."

As they walked from the ice cream shop, sharing each other's flavor, Adria felt more relaxed, and hoped they would find a way to have fun like this after they were married. Then in the distance, she noticed a group of people hanging out at the mall's entrance. Out of the corner of her eye, she thought she saw a small child being removed from the door. Within a few seconds, she heard the door open and the words, "Daddy! Daddy!"

Bryson turned to the right to witness his son running to him as fast as he could. He reached down to scoop him up in his arms and at the same time looked at the door to notice Rheta and others surrounding the entrance. Rheta had an angry look on her face. The man beside her looked unhappy as well.

"Hey little man, what's up!" Bryson asked as he gave his son a big hug.

"Daddy, I miss you! Why haven't you come to get me?" Duane asked with an inquisitive look at Bryson.

Rheta opened the door and beckoned Duane to come to her as she was ready to go.

"We gotta go. Are you going to come and visit me in our new place?" Duane asked.

Bryson did not answer but walked his son to the door.

"Hello Rheta," Bryson stated cordially.

"Bryson," Rheta spoke to him with an emotionless voice, ignoring Adria completely.

"Are you going to bring him over on tomorrow? It's our weekend together and we got some great plans!" Bryson asked enthusiastically.

Rheta quickly glanced up at her male friend before responding, "Sure, what time do you want me to bring him by?"

"How about first thing in the morning? I can take him now if you want?" Bryson offered.

"I don't have his clothes ready," Rheta quickly acknowledged. "I'll drop him off tomorrow for breakfast. Let's go now, Duane."

"Bye Daddy," said Duane cheerfully as he walked with his mother. "See you tomorrow!"

"Bye, sport. I am looking forward to it!" Bryson replied.

Bryson and Adria watched the group walk away and get into their vehicle. She and Bryson walked back into the mall area.

"So, do you think she'll show?" Adria asked as she held onto Bryson's hand.

"Not sure. We'll have to wait and see," Bryson responded, shrugging his shoulders. "I have to trust she will bring him by tomorrow like she said," Bryson stated as they strolled through the first level of the mall.

Adria noted Bryson's mood was polite, and she knew he was worried about his son. They found a bench and sat.

"At least Duane was in good spirits. If there was really something wrong, he would not have been able to hide it," Adria suggested. "He sure was glad to see his Daddy."

Bryson leaned over with an elbow on each leg and his chin resting on his clasped hands. He remained silent and just let Adria talk. After a moment, Adria stopped talking and just waited on him. He took a few deep breaths, then sat back.

"Adria, I am going to try and get custody of Duane. I really think Rheta is on drugs and I can't have my son around that. I contacted an attorney, but the process is very slow." Bryson paused briefly before continuing. "I wish I had fought harder for Duane's custody at the onset when Rheta's behavior was the most unusual. It would have been easier for me to get custody then, but I was not ready for the sole responsibility of him. I am not sure how you envisioned when the two of us would have kids and I am not sure this is even fair to ask you, but if I could get full custody in a few months, how would you feel about my decision?" Bryson asked.

"Honestly, it's been on my mind a lot, since the marriage counseling sessions. I suspected all along it would become top priority for us. You know how much I love kids and Duane is your son," Adria added. "I think between the two of us, we could work it out."

Bryson let his shoulder sag.

"It seems all I've done is bring you problems. Are you sure you want to get hooked up with me?" he asked.

"It won't always be easy, because ... well ... it just won't be easy always, but your problems are like my problems, the results of some decision-making from our past," Adria stated. "You love your son, and he loves you... that is the focus right now."

"Yeah, but your past has not interfered with us at all. My past has kept us on our toes!" Bryson commented.

Adria sat in silence as this was the perfect segue for her to speak about her time away from the family. She searched for the words to initiate the conversation.

"Let's pray my past does not surface and cause us problems as it would be harder for us to work through them, Bryson," she said quickly.

Bryson frowned.

"What do you mean?"

Adria paused briefly before continuing.

Adria's Transformation

"There's something I need to tell you," she began, and reminded herself to use her voice. This was the chance she was waiting for. "Remember at the onset of the counseling sessions when Bishop and First Lady talked to us about trust. They discussed the need for us to be honest and not blindside the other with important information that could derail us later, especially if someone else told us."

"Yes," he said with understandable hesitation.

Adria looked down at her hands as she rubbed the palm of her left hand with her right-hand thumb.

"Well, I have not told you a lot about my time away, other than I worked temporary assignments and had a part time job as a cocktail waitress and bartender in a club, right?" Adria confirmed.

Bryson turned to stare at Adria with a slight frown.

"Yes, you mentioned it a couple of times."

"Let's say it was an eye-opening experience for me." Adria added and then took a deep breath. "I was seeing the club owner at the time, though I was in fact, one of his girls and the one he would take to his special parties. That's how I would make extra money at times."

Bryson's eyebrows shot up.

"Doing what?"

"My job was to find the perfect 'gift.' For example, if it was a birthday party, I would wrap it up nicely and place the gift in a bag. He would inspect the bags, complement me on my findings and wrapping and add his own special gift as well. He would give me the money to purchase the gifts and I could keep the change. I would make sure it was beautifully decorated and top notch."

Bryson didn't seem to understand what she was trying *not* to say. She sighed and said, "Bryson, I was in the pharmaceutical business."

"Like in street pharmaceuticals?" he asked, with shock in his voice.

"Yes. I was the gift bearer, and at first, I was not aware of the types of gifts I was giving. However, I soon found out about it."

"How so?"

"The parties were elaborate and there were all these different types of folks in attendance. I did not think anything bad was going on because everything was so very well prepared and decorated. After a while, I just relaxed and enjoyed the surroundings. However, I had to be tested to see how I would react to certain scenarios and that was how I found out about the extra 'gifts'."

"Were you not afraid of the implications of being put in the situation or felt guilty as to what you were doing to others?" Bryson now seemed to grasp the severity of what she did.

"It was not that type of setting. As I stated earlier, the parties were extravagant at a huge residence or setting and there was nothing in my mind to feel guilty about. I learned how to disconnect myself."

"How?" Bryson further inquired.

"Because of the lifestyle they lived, there was no need for me to feel guilty or sorry for anyone. I was surrounded by some pretty amazing people. And I also found myself involved in some of the most insightful conversations. It became my focus and was why I was the preferred date." Adria stated. "I was very discrete, didn't get overwhelmed by certain situations and could manage my reactions." Adria stopped momentarily. "Also, and most importantly, I was accustomed to keeping secrets. I didn't learn that behavior from the streets." Adria's voice trailed off as she completed the last statement.

Bryson remained silent and stared at the floor for a while longer. After a moment, he simply said, "Humph!"

"You, the distracting front babe, wow!" Bryson stated in disbelief. Adria could detect some incredulity in his voice. "Did you ever get near the product?"

"No, never had to. It was not my job," Adria replied. "I purchased the birthday gifts and prepared the presentation boxes, or bags or whatever I came up with, which could be pretty extravagant. Then the club owner would inspect my work and give his approval. Once we were at the party, I gave the birthday guy or girl their gifts and then enjoyed the festivities," Adria said.

"So, let's see," Bryson said. "You created a job for yourself by being a designer for birthday gifts and parties."

"Yes, they were beautifully decorated, and it became my niche." Adria reminisced.

"I guess it's not like in the movies at all, where everything was all dramatic."

"Not in this case," Adria reflected. "A lot of people just live very quiet lives and you may never know what was going on with them."

"I get it," he said. Then blew his breath out of his mouth and added, "I am shocked because I certainly was not prepared for you to make this kind of announcement. But I do understand there was a clientele for everything." Bryson commented. "Were you a user?"

"No, it didn't appeal to me at all. I had my favorite drinks and they sufficed."

"No one pressured you to join them?" Bryson continued.

"Again, it was not that type of atmosphere," Adria repeated. "No one was forced to do anything."

She looked over at Bryson, who was staring down at the floor.

"I am just trying to take this all in!" Bryson stated aloud. "Have you told your family about this?"

Adria looked at Bryson and momentarily—just for one second—wondered if it was the best idea to share this deep-rooted, dark secret she had hoped was hidden in her past. Now that it was resurrected, she felt strangely worried and anxious. She wondered if Bryson would allow it to remain a memory they no longer needed to discuss.

"No, I have not," Adria responded. "They were already over the top with my decision to be a cocktail waitress at the club. My family considered me an embarrassment and said I had lost my integrity."

"Were you ever going to tell me about it?" Bryson inquired further. "I mean, if it had not been initiated by the marriage counseling sessions?"

"Eventually, yes, as it is a part of my past and not my present life. I have been searching for the words to tell you since we got engaged. This former part of my life does not impact anyone else in my family or you at all. The sessions these previous six weeks have helped me get to this point on the importance of sharing this truth with my husband to be."

Adria had found increased courage in being honest with Bryson and prayed the truth would not backfire on her.

Adria's Transformation

He continued to gaze at Adria and nodded his head slowly as a response.

"Do you feel guilty about the people who you might have hurt then and who are hurting now?" Bryson inquired.

Adria thought of Tiffani, her life, and her eventual demise and how her heart broke in those types of scenarios. "Yes, I have felt all levels of guilt when I am reminded of the people whose lives I have hurt rather than helped," Adria confessed. "All I can do is ask God to forgive me."

Bryson remained quiet, thoughtful, but he didn't ask anything else. Adria took that opportunity to return the conversation where it started. "So, back to your previous question, I think I will be okay with you and Duane and your situation," Adria offered. "As long as I feel like I am first and will not have to always be second and third behind Duane and Rheta."

Bryson reacted affirmatively.

"That's cool! We are cool! I guess I just wanted to make sure we are doing this for the right reasons?" Bryson replied.

"By now, we should know, don't you think?"

"We should," he agreed.

There was a moment of silence between them after Bryson spoke.

"I guess this was really going to happen, huh?" Adria stated.

"Are you getting cold feet, my love?" Bryson teased. "Did I say something to make you feel a little nervousness?"

"I get nervous at times, but no, our lives are never going to be the same. And I look forward to that," Adria stated.

He nodded and said, "I do too," he paused, and then acknowledged, "Thank you for trusting me with your past. I need to take it all in and start digesting everything you shared, but I'm glad you did. Thank you."

Adria didn't realize how much she needed to hear him say that until he did. Then she sighed with contentment and nodded.

Bryson arose and reached out for Adria's hand. Together, they left the mall, holding hands, watching the sights, and commenting on anything that caught their eye.

Chapter 16
The Wedding Day

The morning light was shining through the bay window and splashed warmth on Adria's face. The feeling created a joyful sensation that emanated from her face and moved throughout her entire body. Adria knew before she opened her eyes that this was no ordinary day, but a very, very special one. It was her wedding day and she squealed with joy as she jumped up from the bed.

The alarm clock screamed a festive sound she immediately embraced with all her senses as she danced around the bedroom. She glanced at the clock and picked up the phone to dial her fiancé's number.

"Good Morning, Love!" Bryson answered.

"Good Morning, Sweetie!" Adria responded. "I wanted my voice to be the first voice you heard today!"

"Mission accomplished," Bryson responded.

"I know it's early, but I hoped you would appreciate this gesture," Adria continued.

"I appreciate it a lot!" Bryson offered. "As a matter of fact, I would have been disappointed if you had not called me. It was anticipated."

Adria sat on the side of her bed and knew she was chattering a lot, probably too much, but she couldn't help it. "I am excited and wanted you to hear the excitement in my voice."

"Trust me," Bryson quickly stated, "I'd rather have you excited than *not* excited. You could be crazy at this point!"

"And not to mention driving *you* crazy!" Adria teased.

"My point exactly!" Bryson laughed. Then he became thoughtful. "In just a few hours, less than eight, you and I will be husband and wife," Bryson acknowledged.

"I am elated that it's here and I can't wait to get to the church to marry my Prince Charming. This is MY dream come true and you are in it!" Adria confessed. "And now, my dear husband-to-be, I'd love to continue our chat, but I must go and get beautiful for you, darling!"

"Sure thing; don't let me keep you! You have more things to do today than me!" Bryson remarked.

"Now, that's a true statement. I love you and I'll see you in a few hours!" Adria stated.

CB

"I love you. too!" Bryson replied. He ended the phone call. All he had to do was get him and his son ready, and a quick glance at the clock told him he had some time to relax before awaking Duane. He did not have to be at the barbershop for another hour. He would then gather his son and their belongings and drive to the church. The groomsmen were given the option of dressing at GFCC or arriving fully dressed by 11:00 a.m. – two hours before the ceremony start time.

Adria's Transformation

Bryson hit the treadmill and reminded himself that after today his bedroom would be shared by Adria. This positive thought helped him to complete his run in a more upbeat mood. After he cooled down, he grabbed a bottled water and went into Duane's room to awaken him.

As he moved closer to his son's bed, Bryson thought about how Duane had made significant improvements during the past thirty days. Rheta had simply abandoned Duane. Although he called her every day and left messages, she had not regularly returned his phone calls. Since she dropped Duane off at his Dad's house for a visit, she has only spoken with him once briefly. This was a very unusual behavior for Rheta. She had always made sure she stayed connected and available for Duane no matter what! But he wasn't responsible for her, only Duane, and he was doing his best to make sure he adjusted to his new family.

At times, his son was not entirely happy about his father marrying Adria and questioned Bryson about having to share his father with her. But Bryson talked extensively about the new family unit he was a part of.

Adria also made sure Duane was included as much as possible in all their family activities. When the three of them were together at Bryson's home and enjoying down time, he was invited to sit on the couch with them as they watched a favorite movie or show.

When Duane finally allowed Adria to hold his legs as he lounged and slept during their 'family time', it was an indicator he had moved to another level of acceptance.

The fact that several of Adria's brothers doted on Duane and made him the center of attention at the Darden family gatherings was another positive that helped lessen the impact of Rheta's disappearance on Duane and Bryson was grateful.

Bryson instructed his parents to not allow Duane to attend day care while he and Adria were on their honeymoon. Papa and Mama Darden as well as Francine were also on alert to keep Duane under tight surveillance. He did not want Rheta showing up at the daycare and retrieve their son without Bryson being close by and he not know where he was.

Bryson would explain all of this to Adria at the appropriate time—after they were lounging in their honeymoon spot.

He chuckled as he realized he had not even told Adria where they were going. It had been kept as a surprise and after a while, she stopped asking. He hoped she would be excited about their time spent in St. Lucia. Bryson knew Adria was going to be 'over the top' with joy.

Bryson awakened his son and directed him to become alert and oriented. Duane took a few moments to arouse but eventually got out of the bed to go potty and begin his day.

☙

Adria's drive to the hair salon was uneventful and she managed to only be five minutes late. Her stylist, Suzetta, was waiting for her at the door and offered a big hug and a smile. They chatted and laughed during the hair preparation process, and at precisely 8:30 a.m., Adria walked to her car with her new hairdo wrapped loosely. Next, she would drive to her mother's house to dress. The limousine service was due at 10:15 a.m. Adria promised

Adria's Transformation

Bryson and Miriam she would be at the church no later than 10:30 a.m.

Mama Darden and Francine were waiting for Adria at the front door. Adria walked into the home and was greeted with hugs and kisses before being escorted to her childhood bedroom to dress. Make-up was applied by Dazzle, Francine's friend, and Adria proceeded to get dressed. Once Adria was done, Mama Darden opened the door so Papa Darden could see his 'little girl.'

By 9:45 a.m., Francine slipped on her dress, grabbed her belongings and was ready. She then checked in on Mama Darden to complete her final tasks. By 10:00 a.m. the Darden women were completely attired and ready for the day's wedding activities. The Darden men stopped by on their way to the church to take a few pictures and offer their sister some last-minute advice. When they saw Adria, their eyes glared in amazement. And when 10:17 a.m. came along, Adria and Francine were on their way to the church. Papa and Mama Darden followed closely behind in their own vehicle.

○3

Meanwhile, Bryson had turned into a bundle of nerves. He was so glad to see his Mother and Father's faces when they entered his office. Up to this point, he had held up very well, but during the dressing of Duane, he wondered if Adria was indeed going to show up or leave him at the altar. He knew his source of fear came from the enemy, but the feeling was so strong.

He had Alton give him periodic updates as they were being fed from the Darden brothers. When they finally arrived and stated how beautiful their sister was, he felt somewhat relieved. However, the feeling had not yet totally subsided as he worked himself up into a nervous frenzy.

"Man, you are going to have to calm down," Alton warned. "What has gotten you so hyped?"

"I don't know man; I guess my nerves are getting the best of me!" Bryson reported. He was pacing the floor and fiddling with his tuxedo tie. Then he would walk over to the window to look out before sitting down in the chair to check, for the zillionth time his phone for a text message.

Mr. and Mrs. Kenton checked in on Bryson, who was sitting in his office nervously re-adjusting his tie and whatever else his hands could touch. Mr. Kenton walked over to Bryson to give him a big hug.

"I'm proud of you son! You have handled yourself very well and made your Papa proud." Mr. Kenton offered.

Bryson looked up at his father and said, "Thanks Dad!"

Mrs. Kenton took a few extra moments and allowed her son to sit back in his desk chair.

"Son, you know how much Mama loves you, don't you?" Mrs. Kenton stated as she looked up to see his reaction to her words.

"Yes ma'am," Bryson responded. He felt like a teenager in that moment but appreciated his mom for it.

"I have waited a long time for this day, and I want you to know your Father and I could not be prouder of you. You have made us proud, many times, but today I don't think I have the words to describe how I feel." Mrs. Kenton sighed. "You've been through a lot, and you have held yourself together very well. Like a prince," Mrs. Kenton continued. "Don't you fret, because Adria was

Adria's Transformation

also a princess and I *know* there is nothing the Kenton's and Darden's all can't get through together."

Bryson looked at his mom. She had always known him better than he knew himself at times.

"Adria loves you so much and she can't hide it," she continued. "And I know how much you love her. You've shown it more and more these past few months. You are going to be just fine!"

"Do you think she is going to show up?" Bryson asked quietly in a somewhat joking manner.

Mr. Kenton touched his wife's hand indicating he wanted to answer the question. "It's 10:30 a.m. and I believe when we walk out of this door, we will find she will have arrived and will be sitting in her bridal chamber putting on the finishing touches."

There was a knock on the door to which Bryson responded, "Come in."

The door opened slightly, and Alton stuck his head in. "Hi again, Mr. and Mrs. Kenton. Bryson, I want you to know the limo just pulled in and your bride-to-be is here!"

"How does she look?" Bryson asked with a boyish grin.

"She is gorgeous, man!" Alton stated.

Bryson signaled for him to come in. "Where is Duane?"

"I left him with his uncles, and they are on guard and on point," he reported. "Everyone is in a joyful mood and having a good time. The musicians have arrived and are ready to start playing soon. I think we are all set."

Mrs. Kenton smiled at her son. "You see, I told you everything would work out just fine."

Bryson stood up and nodded. Feeling better, he retrieved his tuxedo jacket from the coat tree and prepared to dress.

☙

Adria was sitting on the bridal sofa with a goblet of ice in her hand. She was having a hot flash brought on by rattled nerves. The miniature oscillating fan Francine purchased was a good investment and positioned close by.

Francine sat comfortably across from her sister in a chair. Mama Darden was at her immediate right.

"We all wondered when you would get to this point," Mama Darden commented. "Just relax, it will be over in a few seconds."

Adria's face was moist with sweat; however, she was breathing more rhythmically now. Just earlier, her breathing was more frantic, and she was blowing loudly and shaking her hands. She did not pace around the room as the dress prohibited her from moving too quickly. She worked hard to remember the stress management techniques she learned and even more diligently to calm herself.

Francine picked up a fan. "You are making me hot!" Her sister began fanning her own face.

"Here, you want some ice?" Adria offered. "It really does the trick for me."

"I envisioned you wanting to bolt to the nearest door when you got to this point," Francine declared and then laughed loudly as she stood to sponge Adria's face.

Adria was quiet but she sighed heavily at Francine's latest remark.

"No, I don't run away from things anymore. I charge head on into them now, face first!"

"Adria, you are not pregnant, are you?" Mama Darden asked critically.

Both Francine and Adria simultaneously laughed as they had this conversation in the limousine. Adria confessed as to how she was sure of a lot of things and that she was NOT pregnant as she had not done anything to GET pregnant.

"No, Ma! Just having a small nervous attack." Adria reassured her mom. "I think I am entitled to one at this point."

"Yes, you are, and you are handling it nicely." Francine stated. There was a knock on the door.

"Come in," Adria responded.

The door opened and Carla and the rest of the bridesmaids were being ushered to the bridal chamber. The bridesmaids looked wonderful in their purple gowns. Walking behind the bridesmaids was one of the photographers, taking candid pictures.

The photographer took pictures of the ladies and the bride. It was an air of extreme excitement everywhere.

Adria turned her attention to Tara. "How's Bryson?" she asked.

"Wondering how you are!" Tara exclaimed.

"You all just missed her nervous moment," announced Francine.

Carla, Yvonne, Val, and Tara focused their attention on Adria who was getting make-up artist attention. The remainder of the bridesmaids also stopped to look over at Adria.

Carla walked over to Adria and sat in front of her." You okay, ladybug?"

"I am much better now," Adria responded as she held her face in the position in which the makeup artist was directing her. "The ice on my pulse points and the ice water got me through it!"

Dazzle draped a sheet over the entire wedding dress and began working on the rest of Adria's face. Meanwhile, the bridesmaids were talkative and chatty. The atmosphere in the room was charged with girl power. Adria had recovered from her nervous attack.

At 12:00 p.m., there came a knock on the door. Papa Darden entered the bridal chamber.

"Hi Honey Bun!" he said.

Adria grinned from ear to ear when she saw her father.

"Hi Poppie! Is it that time?"

"Yes, it is darling," he confirmed. And at that, the bridesmaids were ushered out of the room and into the position to prepare for their entrance. Papa Darden smiled at Adria and said, "Once again, I have to tell you that I have never seen you look so beautiful. You are absolutely stunning!"

"Thanks Daddy!" Adria responded. "I feel much better now."

Papa Darden placed his arm out for Adria, and they prepared to stroll leisurely down the hallway to the sanctuary. Adria was handed her bridal bouquet, composed of miniature white roses laced with baby breath, greenery, and purple and white satins, and they left the room. It was a very short walk and they poised themselves near the interior church doors awaiting the signal from the wedding planner. The two of them wore almost identical radiant smiles that were bathed in love.

Adria's Transformation

Adria heard the music to initiate her march down the aisle. And as she walked, escorted by her daddy, she could not think of a time when her world was so perfectly blessed, and she was this happy!

Adria noticed many of the guests in attendance and smiled brightly. The reaction from Adria's onlookers confirmed she was a beautiful bride. After Adria passed approximately one third of the pews she looked up at Bryson's face. He was smiling.

Deep down inside Adria felt indescribable joy. No one, absolutely no one, could have told her that everything she had been through, cried through, fought through, prayed through, lost, was deprived of, agonized over, and left behind, would set her up for this chance of a lifetime.

YES, she was walking down the aisle with her beloved Poppie.

YES, she was watching as her mother and future in-laws were cheerful and blowing kisses.

YES, she locked eyes with her sister Francine who returned a grin to signal her final stamp of approval on her sister's decision.

YES, when she looked at her brothers, she saw their nods of approval as well.

YES, when she looked at Duane, he was trying to keep from grinning, but she knew he was tickled.

And YES, a few feet from the altar Adria and her father halted, as they were directed in rehearsal on the previous evening. It was Bryson's cue to walk over to Adria. When Bryson dropped to one knee the wedding guests' bursts into applause. He kissed her right hand, Victorian style, and then returned to his standing position. Adria took his arm and held both her Poppies' and Bryson's arm and they walked together to the altar in front of Bishop.

The ceremony was officially beginning. Bishop explained the purpose on this afternoon of the gathering and walked them through the service, including the giving away of the bride and the sharing of vows. Bishop guided them through the ring ceremony and reinforced the significance of the rings and the vows they were reciting on this wedding day. Then prayed the final ritual prayer while the last song was sung by an ensemble. Adria and Bryson were ushered to the prayer bench and Bishop stood before them and prayed.

At the conclusion of the prayer, he offered them words of wisdom. Adria and Bryson returned to the altar and resumed their positions. Bishop then proclaimed, "With the power vested in me, I now pronounce you husband and wife, life partners, life negotiators, chief man and woman in charge of their domain." He then directed Bryson to kiss his bride.

Bryson jokingly rolled his shoulders and popped his knuckles as he prepared for this kiss. Their lips touched and it felt like fire moved between them. The kiss was sweet and loving. After that, Bishop had Adria and Bryson turn to face the congregation to introduce the couple to the church as Mr. and Mrs. Adria Dionne and Bryson Duane Kenton.

Following the ceremony, Adria and Bryson returned to the limo and positioned themselves comfortably for the ride to the reception hall. They sat close together and held hands as they listened to the limousine music chosen just for them.

Adria's Transformation

"Tell me, Mrs. Bryson Duane Kenton, how do you feel now you are no longer a single woman?" Bryson jokingly asked Adria.

"I was about to ask you the same question to see if you are having problems with no longer being a single man," Adria asked, flirting with her new husband. "I have never, ever been this happy. This is my dream come true!" Adria leaned closer to Bryson, and they enjoyed a real, passionate 'just married' kiss. The previous kisses were cordial and respectful; however, this kiss was free and uninhibited. After their lips departed, Adria wiped her lipstick from Bryson's lips and mouth area.

"I love you Bryson", Adria said passionately.

Bryson placed his hand under Adria's chin to lift it slightly. He looked deeply into her eyes to fully view the love she was wearing so freely this afternoon.

"I love you too, my sweets! How about...," then he kissed her lightly—"We"—he kissed her again—

"Totally skip the reception"—he kissed her yet again—"And go directly to the hotel to start the honeymoon. I am not hungry anyway?" Bryson suggested.

"Why not?" Adria agreed. "I don't think they will miss us at all!" She responded jokingly as she then leaned over for a few more kisses. "Well, on second thought, they might miss us a little."

"What do you say we attend for about an hour and a half and then we say our goodbyes?" Adria suggested. "Then I get you all to myself!"

They arrived at the reception and partook of the activities prepared for them. Pictures were taken and guests were greeted. Adria and Bryson had dinner, performed the cutting of the cake and drinking from each other's goblets ceremonies before returning to their seats to receive toasts from the matron of honor and the best man.

Francine was directed to offer her toast first. She stood with the cordless microphone and walked towards Adria and Bryson.

"You two are a lovely couple and Sis, I have never seen you this happy, ever. My prayer, and I plan to pray it often, is that you always carry a part of this moment with you as it is the kind of memory that will carry you through all types of situations. Bryson, now you take good care of my sister, you hear me? I love you both!" Then she raised her crystal goblet to complete the toast. The wedding party and guests raised their glasses and drank to accept Francine's toast.

Adria's eyes filled with tears as to how much Francine had grown to accept Bryson. Today she showed her feelings of love and care that warmed Adria's heart.

Francine then passed the microphone to Alton who stood beside her. Alton cleared his voice.

"Bryson and Adria this is indeed such a great privilege for me to offer a toast to the two of you today. I have known Bryson for a long time and have never seen him so happy. I am really glad to see my friend get to this point IN HIS LIFE. Now I don't have to be jealous of him being single ANYMORE!" Alton added and laughed at himself, and the reception guests joined in with his humor. "Just keeping it real, dawg. Seriously, my prayer is that you keep God first in your life and allow Him to lead you through all your circumstances and you will reach all your dreams. Adria, he's in your hands now and I trust you will take good care of my brother. Bryson, I

Adria's Transformation

am proud of you man!" Then he lifted his glass to complete the toast.

The guests lifted their glasses once again to drink their beverage before applauding at the conclusion of Alton's toasts.

The reception continued with the bridal bouquet and the garter tosses and photographs. Finally, the emcee announced that the newlyweds were ready to depart the scene and start their lives together. Two cordless microphones were placed beside the couple for their usage. Adria and Bryson stood to thank their guests and prepare for their recessional.

"I don't have enough words to thank God, my family, and friends for helping to make this day a dream come true for us. I will always cherish and love every moment. Do pray for us as we strive to be the man, woman, couple, and family God called us to be! We love you all!" Adria said.

Bryson raised his microphone to begin his words. "I agree with everything my new bride has spoken today. God's been so good to us, and we will always be grateful for these bountiful blessings. Thank you all so much and May God bless you!" Bryson signaled the DJ and the music started.

Upon cue, the couple began to sing a song written by Bryson for this occasion. This was the very tune that was inspired by their confessed love for each other many months earlier, on the night they became a couple. This melody, like their lives, have progressed through their scenarios and taken many iterations. The song was a true replica of how their love had grown to this place. The delivery of the tune was passionate and when it concluded, the guests were at their feet with thunderous applause. Bryson and Adria stood close holding hands until the last note was played.

Bryson and Adria said their 'thank you's' and returned the microphones to the table. They prepared to exit the reception. As Adria and Bryson approached the door, they jumped over the broom and left their wedding reception in the capable hands of their family, friends, and the wedding planner.

Adria and Bryson re-entered the limousine.

"I think our song was a big hit!" Bryson acknowledged. "Maybe we ought to do that more often?" He asked as he looked over at Adria with a big smile. "What do you think?" Bryson then locked his hands into hers as he spoke.

Adria grinned and then snuggled as close as humanly possible to her new husband. "That song was very special."

"Do you think we could do it... sing, together again?" Bryson continued, "I mean, we might be onto something very special here, my bride!"

"We could certainly do that again!" Adria responded lovingly as she continued to reflect on her wonderful wedding day. She wrapped her arm around Bryson's waist and laid her head on his shoulder.

The fifteen-minute ride to the hotel was filled with music, joy, and laughter. Adria and Bryson exited the limousine, and the bell captain opened the doors for them. The luggage had been loaded onto the luggage carrier and sent to their rooms earlier. Adria and Bryson stopped at the reception area to pick up the room key. Once inside the bridal suite, Bryson located the "*Do Not Disturb*" sign and placed it on the door.

We Thank God for Second and Third Chances

Dr. Paula Y. Obie

Acknowledgements

First and foremost, I want to thank God for His unfailing love and for giving me this gift and my purpose. My goal is that this and upcoming works continue to give you the glory because you are an awesome God. May others believe in the gifts you have given them and not hesitate when the opportunities are offered.

Second, to the three Women of God, Andrea, Ruth, and Victoria, who I am convinced are my guardian angels walking around on this earth, I just want to take a moment to say thank you. I am forever grateful for your love and passion for literacy, reading and writing that is so completely refreshing. I am so elated that our paths crossed and that we were able to meet and work together to make this dream come true. I can't thank you enough for your willingness to coach me through this process. Your words of encouragement, your prodding, your ability to push me further into the gifting was everything I needed. To God Be The Glory!

Lastly, to my family and friends, who are a constant source of inspiration. It was and are our experiences that first spoke gently to my heart and then empowered me to sit down at the keyboard. Romans 8:28 is one scripture that places everything into perspective for me, "And we know that in all things God works for the good of those who love him, who have been called according to his purpose." (NIV)

Never stop believing!

About The Author

Dr. Paula Y. Obie grew up in a small-town in North Carolina and she is the only female born in a family of eight siblings to Elder Samuel B. Obie and the late Reverend Joyce L. Obie.

In her early life, there was an abundance of love, music, laughter, sports, friends and—of course—church. It was her church upbringing though sometimes was extremely complicated, that kept her grounded even when she struggled with her life's journey.

At a young age, her mother passed; however, before she transitioned, Paula spent many days and nights with her at the hospital. In her conversations to prepare her for life without her mother, she would encourage her to, "Not be like them," and she would call names. She also encouraged her to, "Not let anyone buy you, you are not for sale".

These words were vehicles to drive her through many life scenarios. Writing, after this transitional life experience, became a tool she used for sporadic journaling and venting. Later, professionally, she used it as an operational and developmental business management writing tool. In 2008, Paula was encouraged to write her faith journey, with the end result of being a love story.

"I laugh at the power of God, who can take a tragical life and transform it into love! Only God can perform that miracle."

Paula loves spending time with her family, walking along the beach and just sitting and looking at the spectacular sea for hours.

CPSIA information can be obtained
at www.ICGtesting.com
Printed in the USA
BVHW041132150223
658561BV00001B/2